Decisions

by Stephanie Dunlap Holloman
Buard Family Series – Book 1

BUARD FAMILY SERIES – Book 1

DECISIONS

Copyright © 2017 by Stephanie Dunlap Holloman

All rights reserved. No part of this book may be reproduced or transmitted in any form or by any means without written permission of the author.

This is a work of fiction. Names, characters, businesses, places, events and incidents are either the products of the author's imagination or used in a fictitious manner. Any resemblance to actual persons, living or dead, or actual events is purely coincidental.

ISBN 978-1-947741-09-6

Kingdom Publishing LLC
Odenton, MD 21113
Printed in the United States of America

Dedication

To my sweet, strong, sexy husband Frank, thank you for believing in and supporting me; you always knew you were going to be the steadying influence in my life – God is faithful!

To Momma's Babies: Tajia/Mush, Jadon/Bean-Bean, Anique/Doona, and my granddaughters Analisa/Youbaby and Katherine/Yumbaby.

Jacquelynne and Marilyn – The dynamic Dunlap women who raised me.

To Ravan, Qai, Kazzie, & Tanya – the endurance of Family!

To Michelle and Barbara – my best friends.

To my Dad – Ronald Kelley, who loves ya baby?!

Hey Granny/Debbie Simms! How you like the book?

To Deena/Boo and Terronda – Your girl did it.

To Luz/Chica and Aisha/Faison – can we get in trouble together?!

To Delores and Taara and Melaine – I've jumped in… swim with me….

To Joy-Bells – Thank you for being in my life!

Dana, my Sands, thank you for being there!

And to all My Sisters contemplating the turns and twists of their lives – sometimes it's all in how you're looking at it.

Saadri Isaure Buard Weston

January 28, 1965

Power

in the might of

the hand

who planned

and guided

the manifestation of

the magnificence

within me.

And I stand ready

to explore

and conquer

and understand

and experience

and live.

<h1 style="text-align:center">Chapter 1</h1>

1982

Summer draped itself in New York City verve and pranced under the steel sentinels positioned to bathe the neighborhood's perimeter in yellowed light. In the distance, music blared from a DJ's jam as traffic lights changed with programmed synchronicity that sent cars and pedestrians speeding toward diverse destinations. Consumer enticements flashed in neon signs. Lively commentary over a card game instigated accusations and challenges that forecasted an abrupt and violent end. Young women sauntered by groups of admiring young men. A couple argued for all to hear. Dice crashed against building walls amidst animated reactions. Brooklyn's East New York, Brownsville neighborhood, embodied a tempo that drew many into its bustle.

Najid Raenier rested his muscular frame against a car outside the building where he resided with his parents. A group of four young men gathered around him. Najid surveyed as the group discussed business. His silent and authoritative bearing appealed to females attracted to the New York roughneck type; yet, he was different. Behind the unflappable bearing was a young man who grappled with frustrated longings. He yearned for someone special to expel the taunting emptiness that dogged him daily. Najid bided his time in the rat race; an inaudible sigh refocused his attention to the crew.

"Yeah, so I told that kid if he didn't come through, there would be consequences. I'm a chill right here, he'd better come to me with mines." Tyreek Daniels was the group's loud mouth who also had the means to back up any threat. Equally reliable in resolving threats was

Dana Murphy, the other young man involved in the conversation. Dana's frequent nods indicated the beginning of a plan to toughen the standards; after all, he was the group's enforcer. Two others, David Jones and Eric Nixson, completed the group of five who held highest rank in the underworld of Brownsville.

Najid shifted and the conversation ended when the group saw his younger brother approach. As specified by their leader, the group could hang out with Rasheen Raenier but never include him in their business dealings. They greeted him with hearty daps and the customary "Yo Rah! What's up?!" then resettled and spoke concerning various activities within their building.

Rasheen interjected, "Yo D! What's up with you and Trinette?"

David returned his question, "Why? What's up?"

Rasheen continued, "I wanted to know if she was still 'you' cause I saw her out in Manhattan with that dude Chris from Tilden. They looked real comfortable with one another and last I knew she was 'you'. So...what's up?"

David chewed his bottom lip, a habit known in the circle to mean trouble. Najid regarded the scene coolly. David offered, "It's about to be something."

Rasheen nodded his head along with the others as he spoke, "I figured as much. Might as well hear it from someone in your crew, you know?"

David extended his hand toward Rasheen, "Good looking out man."

"Ty, your boy is here." Najid's baritone commanded the space. He nodded toward the approaching lumber of the young man Tyreek spoke of earlier. The guy was a constant source of irritation to Tyreek, yet he didn't get rid of Jaime as a favor to a close mutual cousin. Jaime nodded, passed the group and walked on a few yards toward a barely patient Tyreek. While the others watched events unfold with the pair,

Najid motioned for Rasheen's attention. They stepped away from the scene and he spoke to his brother, "You know there will be static, don't you?"

Rasheen stared at his brother for a moment. "He didn't need it to get back to him through the grapevine. I can't hang out with dude and—"

Najid stated, "Sometimes you have to see but not see. We don't need unnecessary static and you know them Tilden dudes will 'nut' to back their boy."

Rasheen inquired, "Can't you stay out of it? It's really about him and his girl."

Najid shook his head, "Come on Rah, you know better than all that. You have the brain for the books, that's true, but the street knowledge is important too. If word got back to him that you were hip to what happened, you could have let him know it was between him and his girl. Everything would have been squashed."

Rasheen disagreed, "The static would have still escalated between you and the Tilden crew though."

Najid concurred, "Maybe, but your involvement would have been non-existent."

The brothers ceased conversation as Najid watched Tyreek return to the group. David, Eric and Dana huddled around. "That fool is really making my patience wear thin."

Najid refused to respond as he watched Tyreek's expectant face. Instead he addressed Eric, "How things going with you man?"

Eric had a slight lisp yet, the ladies still favored him. Whereas females were enamored with Najid's take-charge demeanor and rugged features, Eric's classic pretty boy looks held them enthralled. "Ace, it's all good. You know I'm getting ready to have a kid. Chianna is going to drop her load in a few more weeks. She's big; I just hope only one pops out."

Dana teased, "Yo! I hope so too for your sake. She won't be no more good after popping out two babies!"

Eric's face reddened, "Keep your mouth off my girl!"

Najid looked past the group and spoke to settle them, "D, here comes your girl. Don't nut out here man."

An attractive female threesome walked down the street toward the group. Trinette Lewis walked in the middle of the trio. Angelina Diaz walked to her right; her older sister was Eric's girlfriend Chianna. Najid emitted a low growl as he looked to Trinette's left and into the face of Saadri Buard. Rasheen heard his brother's response and smiled. He covertly teased, "You still have that thing for Saadri, Ace? Why haven't you tried to push up on her by now?"

Najid watched Saadri. "She wasn't ready for me." His attraction for Saadri lasted over three years but he never approached her because he knew she was three years his junior, a year behind Rasheen. Najid quickly manipulated the numbers in his head. "She's finishing high school this year isn't she?" Rasheen nodded and knew Najid had given himself a green light.

The calm evaporated when David bounded toward Trinette. He grabbed her arm, yanked her toward him throwing the young women flanking her off balance. Najid stood from his perch on the car, "D! Cool out!" David regained his temper and pulled Trinette away from the larger group. Najid walked over and spoke to the ladies, "Are you two okay?"

Saadri nodded mutely while Angelina answered, "Yeah, thanks for asking Ace. What's up with that?!" She motioned derisively toward David.

Eric walked over and responded, "It's cool. Where's Chi?"

Angelina moved to stand beside Eric, "She's probably home eating." They stepped away to talk.

Saadri didn't know whether to stand in place or continue walking. The company she suddenly found herself in made her nervous. Many unfavorable stories circulated the neighborhood about the exploits of the seemingly small band. She witnessed on a few occasions how others miscalculated the group's connections and tried to move in on them. The support they managed to amass was amazing, as swarms of battle ready young men rallied to their aide. Najid was the most frightening and enigmatic of the group. More myths traveled about his single-handed feats than of the group of five together. She never realized how handsome he was; then again, she'd never taken the time to study his features. He looked at her with a lopsided grin, almost daring her to make the next move. Saadri quickly scanned the remaining faces and found the friendly smile of Rasheen, "Hey Rah-Rah, what's up?!"

Rasheen laughed as Saadri purposely ignored Najid. He knew his brother would wear the unsuspecting young woman down. Enough drama would occur between them sooner or later. Rasheen decided to lighten the mood by teasing her, "I wondered if you were going to speak. You're looking good. What are you doing out here tonight? You're usually in the house."

Najid watched the exchange and wondered when Saadri's voice changed from the squeaky staccato of her younger years to the smooth alto cadence she used with his brother. He felt his pulse race as he watched her.

Saadri moved away from Najid as she answered Rasheen, "It's better out here than in a hot house. Besides, I'm hanging out with my girls here-"

The heated exchange between David and Trinette interrupted all conversation. Trinette screamed at David for secretly seeing a girl who lived in nearby Van Dyke housing and threatened to see Chris again. David's hand shot into the air when Najid's baritone commanded, "This is not the time or the place D!"

Dana and Tyreek quickly moved to separate the couple. Najid gave a silent command; Eric walked over and spoke quietly to David. David began to gain control.

Saadri watched the events with a mixture of anger and nausea. She walked to Trinette, "Are you okay? Did he hurt you?" Trinette shook her head as Najid's voice interrupted further interchange between them.

"Trinette, you cool? He won't do anything out here. Maybe you should go on home or -"

Saadri rounded on Najid, "Why should she go home?! He is the one with the problem!" She pointed an accusing finger toward David before continuing. "What's all of this about him not doing anything here and this not being the time or place? What? Is it fine for him to hit her indoors? Who are you anyway? Who gave you the authority to deem the time and place of events?"

Rasheen walked up and tried to calm Saadri with a soothing hand to her shoulder but Saadri shrugged him off. "Everyone is scurrying around here obeying your every command like you're the Godfather or something."

Najid spoke in a low voice, only Rasheen and Saadri could hear him, "You've changed over the years. You weren't so outspoken before."

Saadri narrowed her eyes, "Well, you haven't changed a bit. You're still a thug. I didn't like you then and I don't like you now." No one made a sound.

Najid smiled, "But you will." He couldn't pinpoint when she developed such fire but it was there now. Even in her anger she oozed femininity and he liked that.

Saadri, irritated by his smile, geared up to unleash when Rasheen broke in. "Saadri, let's take a walk." She acquiesced.

Najid watched his brother run interference as he held Saadri about the shoulders. Rasheen guided her down the street towards their building's entrance. No female had ever spoken to him the way Saadri had and normally he would have been boiling. Not this time, however, he noted an accent, a hint of something in her speech he could not pin down. Not once did she use profanity, something he abhorred for women to practice. Najid had his pick of females in Brownsville but he didn't indulge himself. He preferred a lady and they were few and far between in the concrete jungle where he lived. Najid knew Saadri was different. The difference stoked the low burn of longing in his gut. Did he have a right to think he could have something special with Saadri? Najid willed himself to take the chance. He knew the decision meant more than dating a girl who had him enamored over the last three years; Najid took a deep breath and prepared to begin a chain of events that would drastically alter his world. He leaned against a nearby car and watched with interest as Rasheen and Saadri turned back toward the group.

Najid caught her gaze and held it. Saadri walked forward until she stood boldly in front of him. He noticed her thin lips, shoulder length hair, almond-shaped eyes, and slender build – but it was the color of her skin that undid him; under the yellowed streetlight, her skin's caramel coloring simply glowed. Candy. That's what her skin reminded him of - the sweet caramel that hugged an apple on its first dip, rich and creamy and smooth. Najid swallowed and maintained eye contact. He admired her fire. She was a lady but she was no push over. He waited for her to make the first move.

Saadri perceived Najid wanted to intimidate her. She began in an even tone, her temper held in check. "I would like to apologize for my outburst. I was not happy about what I saw. I also didn't mean to be insulting toward you. I don't know you well enough to say I don't like you."

Najid smiled, "I accept your apology and I'm glad to know you're such a lady. I look forward to getting to know you better. I think once you can make an informed opinion of me you definitely won't be able to say you don't like me. What are you doing tomorrow night? I'm sure the lovebirds can get it together and come along. The others can scrounge up dates too."

Saadri understood his challenge; again, she would not be intimidated. Saadri spoke with confidence she felt at the moment, "If I am supposed to be getting to know you then why so many others around?"

Najid grinned, "That's fine, we can go alone. I wanted you to be comfortable. How about I pick you up at seven tomorrow?"

Saadri watched Najid studying her face, "Seven will be fine."

He stood, "I'll be at your apartment promptly then, thank you for agreeing to go out with me."

Saadri couldn't figure out how or why she allowed herself to be baited. Her mother was going to have a fit. Lost for words, she broke eye contact and addressed the group, "Well, have a good night everyone." The damage was done and there was no sense in putting her foot further into her mouth, it was best she went inside.

Rasheen smiled, "Goodnight Saadri." Everyone else said goodnight. Saadri caught sight of David and Trinette snuggled against a nearby light pole and shook her head. Najid obviously knew more than she did about affairs of the heart. On that point alone, his being the leader was well deserved. When she turned to leave, Najid's baritone ensnared her.

"Goodnight Candy."

Saadri turned, "My name is Saadri, Najid, Saadri Buard."

Najid smiled, "I'm aware of that. You're Candy to me though."

Saadri shook her head, "I'm not even going to ask why," and continued to their building.

Najid laughed to himself as he watched her walk away. In time she would know why she was his Candy, and his she would be.

Saadri entered her first floor apartment, checked on her mother and flopped on her bed. She had to admit to the spark of excitement she felt while verbally sparring with Najid. He was far more intelligent than she gave him credit for. Maybe… who was she kidding? They lived in totally different worlds; he was not Prince Charming. Saadri prepared for a shower and the fallout from her impetuous decision.

Chapter 2

The day progressed like a slow, torturous nightmare as Saadri listened to her mother's ranting for what seemed like the thousandth time. "For the life in me, I don't know what has gotten into you Saadri Isaure Buard! What would possess you to accept a date from that boy?! You know what he does! He's a hoodlum and you are not being cute trying to go out with him."

"Mon mon I wasn't trying to be cute. I hadn't even planned on going out with him. Things happened so fast, and before I knew it, I was accepting a date from him."

Ellen Weston shook her head, "You see, that's what I mean! You're playing with fire. You have been raised in the church and that boy is not someone you need to involve yourself with."

Saadri sighed; she never liked upsetting her mother. She knew Ellen was fearful of the same thing happening to her… Damas Buard was a handsome Louisiana Creole man who pursued Ellen for six months on the campus of Xavier University before she finally consented to allow him to date her. A year and a half later, she became pregnant with Saadri. Fed up with Damas' philandering ways, she left Louisiana and returned to New York and her disappointed parents in spite of Damas trying to marry her. She refused to put herself through a life of sharing him with other women. When she found out about his fathering two other children it helped cement her stance.

Although she wanted no more to do with him, she was thankful that neither he nor his mother Mazie would allow her to remain separated from them. A look at her daughter reminded Ellen she did not have to suffer through Saadri's teen years alone. "Maybe I should call your father. If you won't listen to me, I know he can get through to you."

Saadri watched Ellen adjust her tired, thinning body on a kitchen chair. She wondered, again, how long her mother would be with her. Ellen suffered from kidney disease and recurrent bouts of cancer. Dialysis treatments twice a week, a recently completed round of chemo, and many prayers kept her alive. Saadri spoke, "I'll be careful Mon mon. It's one date. I don't have to go out with him anymore after this. Please don't call Pe'r." Her father, Damas, or as she called him Pe'r was the source of her Creole background and one she definitely did not want to talk to about dating.

Ellen focused her weary eyes on her daughter's beautiful face, Damas' face. "Baby, I tried to teach you so many things about life. It's almost been unfair to you but I never knew how much time I would have with you. I want you to keep your eyes open and be very careful. You want more than the projects and raising a baby on your own for your life. I would like for you to be married with a family and away from here whether or not I see it come to pass. Your father wants that for you too. I think you should go to Texas with him once I am gone."

"Mon mon, I already told you. I am going to make my life here in New York. Pe'r and I will still have our relationship. Besides, there are more opportunities here in New York."

Ellen sighed, "The Bible speaks of wisdom and following instruction. I didn't raise you in the church for you to turn your back on what you were taught. You're getting ready to make a choice that's going to be hard to live with Saadri."

Saadri bristled, "Mon mon, I'm going out on a date, that's all."

Ellen slapped her hand against the wooden kitchen table, "Don't play with me girl and don't fool yourself! You like that boy because if you didn't you would not have agreed to go out with him. You're attracted to that wild side in him and it's going to get you in trouble. Don't think I'm going to sit back and turn a blind eye to what you're doing because you're about to be eighteen and just about out of school. Now our situation is different and I'm not going to spend time I don't have putting you out or fighting with you. From one woman to the next, you sure better know what you are doing!"

Saadri sighed heavily; no one won an argument against Ellen Weston. She should have been a lawyer. Instead of voicing her thoughts, Saadri answered with, "Okay Mon mon. I'll be really careful. I need to go and make myself ready." Ellen nodded as Saadri walked toward her bedroom.

By ten after seven Saadri was in her mother's bedroom helping her put on a robe to meet Najid. They carefully walked through the short hallway to the living room.

Najid saw Ellen's disconcerted look and knew she, like so many others, had already made up her mind about him. Nevertheless, he stood and smiled as Ellen and Saadri made their way toward him. He saw Ellen's condition and walked toward the kitchen table where he pulled out a seat and helped Ellen sit down. Ellen flinched at his touch but Najid continued. He determined to show Ellen nothing but respect and kindness as his elder and Saadri's mother. "How are you tonight Miss Weston? I'm Najid Raenier."

Saadri smiled as his deep voice filled the small eating space. She especially liked the way he pronounced his last name – Renyeah. It was then that Saadri realized it wasn't Najid's wild side that attracted her; it was his poise and inner strength. Intuitively, Saadri knew there was more to the hardened veneer Najid showed the world. She wanted to get beneath the surface, for there she was sure was a man of substance.

Ellen looked up at the young man, surprised by the strong baritone of his voice and stammered. "Call… me Miss Ellen, Najid. Thank you for helping me." Then she saw the way Saadri looked at the young man and the stammer left. "I want my daughter home by midnight. That should give you two plenty of time on your date. How old are you anyway? I see you around in the evenings, you work in the daytime?"

The barrage of questions Ellen fired embarrassed Saadri. "Mon mon, please give him a chance to respond."

Ellen cut a look at her daughter to keep silent. Saadri lowered her eyes, as she made sure her mother was comfortably in the seat.

Najid was impressed with the fact that in spite of her obvious illness, Ellen Weston was very much in control of her household. He was equally impressed with the amount of respect Saadri showed her mother. He placed a hand on each woman's shoulder before he spoke.

Ellen was again surprised by the young man's adroit maneuver as he captured their attention. No wonder he was the leader of the pack. Saadri was definitely out of her league with him. Ellen's musings were interrupted by his response.

Najid drew Ellen into his direct gaze and never wavered as he answered every question she asked of him. "I'm twenty and will be twenty-one in February. I work on Wall Street during the day. I have had that job since I finished high school. I also take night classes at Baruch in finance. I'm taking a break this fall because I'm going through training at my job. Your daughter will be home by midnight, thank you for allowing me to take her out."

Ellen's eyes widened, her mouth hung open. In his answer, he made sure to address the doubts Ellen had about his worthiness of dating her daughter. Najid was definitely a force to be reckoned with. But Ellen was ready, "Twenty, you say? Saadri is seventeen and I want her back in here by eleven instead." Najid nodded and reached for her hand. She shook his extended hand and watched as he ushered Saadri out of the front door. Her daughter had totally missed the subtleties in their exchange, Ellen was sure of it. She then prayed for the Lord to watch over her daughter. One thing she surmised about Najid Raenier was that he would always maintain control – he was Saadri's Damas.

As Saadri locked her front door, Najid stood near; she could smell his cologne. She turned and met him head on. Najid smiled and Saadri swallowed and watched him for a moment. Najid returned her stare and the two seemed to be engaged in a match of wills. Saadri began to feel a little light headed and wondered if her mother's words were true. She certainly never met anyone like Najid Raenier.

Having been in the apartment and then standing in front of her, Najid was able to take in her features: light caramel skin; long brown hair with blond highlights to the middle of her back; almond, hazel eyes; thin eyebrows; a pouty lower lip; thin upper lip; straight nose with slight flare at the nostrils; high pronounced cheekbones; dimpled smile; squared jawline; and very slim. He was enthralled. Najid looked into her golden brown eyes and was convinced he wanted to be important in her life. Yet, she watched him with so much trepidation; he wanted to reach out and embrace her. Najid felt the need to make everything perfect for her; judging from her mother's condition, Saadri didn't have it easy. "Are you ready to go?"

He extended his arm toward the staircase and Saadri moved in the direction. Najid kept his hand on the small of her back. He spoke softly in her ear as they walked out of their building, "I'm glad you said yes to us going out and getting to know one another. We'll have a good time this evening, I'm sure of it."

Saadri felt as if she were floating. Najid's cologne and baritone were wrecking her sense of reality. She answered him but felt as if she were outside herself. "I believe we'll have a good time too."

The couple was oblivious to the stares of shock, dismay and envy emanating from various residents and bystanders. Najid walked closely beside Saadri so no one mistook whether they were together. He viewed her dreamy expression and hoped Saadri was responding to him the way he responded to her. Several people spoke as they walked down the path away from the building's entrance and they returned greetings. When the couple rounded the corner and prepared to cross the street, Najid slipped his hand into Saadri's. He was elated when she didn't resist or release it once they safely crossed to the other side. They walked toward the Rockaway Ave. train station at a medium gate.

"What would you like to know about me first?" Najid began.

Saadri answered with, "I think you already know you blew me away with your Wall Street job and night classes at Baruch."

Najid laughed, "Not bad for a thug, huh?"

Saadri looked up to his five foot ten inches from her own five feet and two inches. "I apologized for that Najid."

He shook the hand he was holding, "I was joking about it. It's no big deal. Tell me, what do you plan on doing when you graduate?"

Saadri enjoyed holding Najid's hand but covered her reaction with a prompt answer, "I want to stay home and go to college. I applied to CUNY for Queens and Brooklyn, and to NYU. I would like to work for a publishing house or a newspaper."

Najid smiled and Saadri noticed how it softened his handsome but hardened features. "You know your mind. I like that. You look really pretty tonight, like the lady that you are."

Saadri looked down at her off white rayon ankle length skirt and pale pink, rayon, shell blouse and muttered, "Thank you."

Najid laughed aloud, "Oh man! You're shy?! After the way you told me off last night, I wouldn't have thought you were shy."

Again Saadri looked up, "That was rare. I was upset because David was going to hit Trinette. I don't handle that type of drama very well."

Najid stopped their stride and turned Saadri to face him. "That's because you're a lady. You should never have to get used to things like that." Saadri looked at Najid's potent dark eyes and nodded. Something about the self-assurance he exuded took Saadri's bravado away. They continued walking to the train station in a comfortable silence. Saadri could feel the authority that was so much part of Najid filter through her and wondered on the type of relationship they could have.

Najid never let her hand go, even when he paid for their tokens. They continued up the stairs and stood on the platform waiting for the train "So, what do you want to see tonight?"

"Whatever you have planned is fine with me."

Najid nodded, "So, you can be agreeable, huh?"

Saadri playfully pushed his nearest arm, "I'm not that bad am I?"

Najid eyed her appreciatively, "No, you're not bad at all." He immediately regretted his forward gesture for Saadri lowered her head. To lighten the mood, he quickly added, "You want to know about bad," and told her stories about he and his brother growing up. Soon she laughed as Najid spun yarns about the mischievous early years of the Raenier boys. The train wasn't in sight but Saadri didn't mind as she found Najid's company to be extremely pleasant. He was nothing like the 'Godfather' image he portrayed in the neighborhood. She mustered up the nerve to ask him about his neighborhood image when she saw his body visibly stiffen. He pulled her into his chest as if to protect her from imminent danger. Saadri stared up into his face with a questioning gaze. Najid returned it with an authoritative look; he had the distinct ability to communicate without uttering a word. Saadri knew something was not right so she moved her body as close to his as possible. When she felt him stiffen, she spoke, "Najid?"

He whispered, "Shhh baby, it's okay. Just stand next to me and I'll watch for the train."

Saadri moved her body slightly; out of her periphery she could see a group of guys ascend the other end of the platform. She silently prayed everything would be all right. Her mother's words came back to her full force. She played with fire; Najid was out of her league. She began to want the date to be over and not see him again. He attracted and charmed Saadri to the extent that it was easy to forget the dangerous side of life he walked on. No, she couldn't prove anything concrete but being out in the dark streets of East New York or anywhere else in Brooklyn meant something unsavory could go down at any moment. She couldn't dismiss that side of him and fall into his web of gentleness.

Najid sensed her withdrawal and enveloped her in a protective embrace. When he gathered Saadri, the top of her head fit beneath his chin. She felt so right in his arms. He looked at how her bare shoulders regally stood out from her tank top blouse and smiled. He wanted to tell her he could love her and they could be happy together. However, the moment wasn't right; he had to keep an eye out for the Tilden crew at the other end of the platform. He could and would protect them if necessary. He watched their movements.

The crew seemed oblivious to their presence on the platform until Chris Williams spotted Najid and Saadri. Chris looked at the way Najid moved his arm possessively around Saadri's petite figure, took his cue and moved on. He said something to the others because they all turned around and looked at the couple. One by one, each of the young men nodded their acknowledgement of Najid's presence. Najid nodded in return. He could see the train's lights at the Junius Street station and he let Saadri know that fact. Saadri sighed; glad they could finally get to their destination. She was never aware that Najid moved just enough for the others to recognize he was prepared to handle any conflict.

Chapter 3

Najid worked overtime with lighthearted stories and plenty of good conversation to get Saadri to move past the platform incident mentally.

Saadri arched a brow toward Najid when the train doors closed at Forty-Second Street. He smiled, he could watch her unceasingly. "A penny for your thoughts."

"Don't act like you don't already know some of my thoughts," she laughingly nudged him.

He stood and pulled her gently from the seat as the train sped along the track. "I wouldn't take you on a date to The Deuce. That's for hanging out with the crew. He led them onto the Fifty-Ninth Street platform and up to the affluence of Manhattan. They ended up seeing "Blade Runner" and Najid was the epitome of a gentleman the entire night. He held her hand during the movie, they shared a bag of popcorn, and afterward they strolled around talking and getting to know one another.

Saadri marveled at the more relaxed and engaging young man. They passed a shoe store near Fifty-Third Street and Najid stopped, "Hey Candy, take a look at these, do you like them?" He pointed to a pair of hot pink leather calf-high boots with a ruched look and two and one-half inch heels. "I think you'd look good in them. Let's go inside."

"Wait, those boots are ninty-five dollars. I don't have that kind of money so there's no need to try them on." Saadri made to walk away but Najid prevented her.

"Let's just go inside and let me see them on your feet." He watched her a moment and smiled. Saadri felt her heart flutter. She went inside and felt him communicating with her while they were in the store. Though he didn't say a word she knew he wanted her to cooperate. She was shocked when he paid cash for the boots.

Najid took the bag from the clerk, led them out of the store, and suggested they walk down to Forty-Eighth Street where he could treat her to clams on the half shell. "This is my gift to you Candy, and before you ask, I bought these boots with my hard earned pay check. I want you to have something nice from me simply because I think you should have nice things and I didn't like some of what you had to experience last night. It's my gift to you and I will be insulted if you don't take it."

The dichotomy of the night sent Saadri's thoughts in many directions. "How do you live a double life? The Bible says you can't serve two masters."

Najid looked at her thoughtfully, "Do you still go to church a lot?"

Saadri answered, "Yes, I am there every Sunday and most Tuesday nights."

Najid shook his head, "That's what makes you so different. You do know you're not like the other girls out where we live, don't you?"

Saadri disagreed, "I'm just me and I'm not trying to be better than anyone else."

"I know that Saadri, and that's why you are so different. You don't think and act the way most of the girls do out our way. You're a cut above. As for me, I'm a man trying to survive in harsh circumstances."

Saadri responded, "Don't tell me you're going to give me that speech about it being the system that's keeping a brother down. I didn't figure you for that type. You have such a strong personality I think you can do anything you put your mind and energy to."

Najid smiled, "It makes a man feel ten feet tall when his woman has his back. I need you in my corner cause then I know I will be able to go places."

Saadri shook her head, "You don't need me, and you have done pretty well for yourself."

"I want you though. How do you feel about that?"

"You hardly know me Najid. You could only want one thing from me."

"Do you think I'm just noticing you?"

"No."

"You would be right! I've been waiting over three years for you girl. Now you're old enough to be with me and I want you."

Saadri felt the heat of the fire. "Najid, I haven't had time to know you. You've had a head start. I feel overwhelmed by all of this sudden attention."

Najid pulled her closer, "I want you and I am not going to lie about it. But, if you want to go slow then that's cool with me. Just as long as you're mine. So can you give a brother a chance? I already showed you tonight I know how to treat a lady like yourself." Saadri pulled back from the embrace. Najid didn't like it but he knew she needed to proceed slowly.

Saadri figured the best way to handle the powerful young man in front of her was to be direct. "What are you expecting from me?"

He wrapped both arms around her waist and rested his forehead against hers. "To be my lady, Candy."

Saadri inquired, "Why do you keep calling me Candy?"

He didn't hesitate to answer, "You're skin is so smooth and pretty with its caramel color it looks like candy. I can't wait to taste it."

Saadri felt the fire kick up a notch. "Taste it?"

Najid lowered his lips to hers in a kiss that didn't demand much but promised a wealth of possibilities. Saadri's large eyes widened and he knew she wasn't ready for him to do that. Something about her made Najid want to renege on his promise to take it slow, yet he refrained from kissing her again. Najid gave her a reassuring smile then guided them to the raw bar. "Let's go eat."

Saadri found she liked clams as they devoured two dozen. Najid finished one and watched her eat one. "You know, clams are erotic food. They build up the libido."

Saadri almost choked, "Well, I don't need any more because I'm waiting for my husband. If that's what you want from me then we might as well quit while we're ahead."

Najid raised his hand in a peace sign, "I am not expecting anything you're not willing to give. I don't force myself on anyone. What do you expect from me?"

Saadri never hesitated, "To be honest with me. I know I'm not as streetwise as you are but I don't want to be the last to know. If this isn't what you thought it could be then tell me, you will be free to leave, no drama. Just don't run around on me if it's supposed to be about us. Do the right thing."

Najid challenged, "What's the right thing?"

Saadri asserted, "I can't answer that for you Najid. If our definitions are too mismatched then we'll need to leave one another alone."

Najid sat back and looked at her a long while before stating, "You definitely know your mind."

As Najid and Saadri walked down Rockaway Avenue, they held one another around the waist. Saadri marveled at how she went from telling Najid off one night to becoming his woman the next. 'And to think he said it was going to happen!' Saadri realized she wasn't the only one to know his/her mind. Both considered the struggles ahead due to their budding romance as they strolled in a comfortable silence.

Fall 1982

Saadri walked from the train station thinking about the day's class in Black History. Unlike classes she took in the past, her instructor presented the elective in a thought-provoking discussion format. That day they discussed at length the work and philosophy of W.E.B. DuBois. More specifically, they critically analyzed the implications of his 'crabs in a barrel' statement. Immediately Saadri thought about the neighborhood in which she lived and how no one seemed to be able to rise above the ills of urban blight and poverty. What perplexed and saddened her more was that no one seemed to want others to escape the cycle either. Mothers raised children alone and many daughters repeated this by raising their own fatherless children. The few people she knew to escape, left and never returned.

Saadri knew she wanted to be counted among the success stories. The future of a life in East New York did not appeal to her. She thought about Najid and what role he would play in her realizing this dream. She desperately prayed he would not hinder her in any way. They spent a great deal of time together over the past two months yet he never mentioned wanting to leave. As much as he grew on her, Saadri would not let Najid cause her to underachieve.

Saadri grew tired as she crossed Blake Avenue and approached her building. Every day seemed like a chore when she had to pass nosy neighbors, trifling, jealous girls, and fresh, disrespectful males. This day, the chore loomed more arduous than usual as the mild late-September afternoon permitted all who could to be outside. She rounded the corner and met a yard full of crabs seated on benches and leant against the fence that led to the building's entrance. Saadri spoke out of respect she was taught to the older, bitter women of her building. She sighed when she thought about how they huddled together and predicted doom on all of the younger residents. Unfortunately, many of their predictions came true.

She spied one of the young men straighten from the fence and knew drama was about to begin. Gary Stratton blocked Saadri's path, he tried to get her attention unsuccessfully for two years. "So Miss Brainiac, where you going with all them books?"

Saadri stopped and stared him in the eye. There was no sense in addressing his snide mocking of her intelligence. Stupidity did as it was. She learned long ago to ignore the unfavorable comments while striving to excel at the prestigious Ft. Greene Prep High School in spite of the jealousy of others. "I was trying to mind my business and go in my house if you don't mind Gary. You're in my way."

Gary sucked his teeth and looked her up and down. "What else is in your way? Or should I say, who else?"

Saadri felt her stomach lurch; she pondered slapping Gary but knew it would have no effect. His ignorance wasn't worth a show of emotion. "I don't see how what or who could be any of your business Gary. Now I would like to go into the building if you don't mind."

When Saadri tried to step around him, he blocked her path again. "Yeah, I do mind. I ain't good enough for you but you mess with Ace? You think he's any better? You think you his only girl? At least I would have only been with you."

Saadri sucked her teeth and stepped around Gary. She held no patience for his silly or malicious ways, especially in front of a yard full of gaping people. As she continued toward the door, an unfamiliar young woman approached her. Saadri saw her, knew it wasn't a social call and thought, 'What now?'

"So you're Saadri. Well I'm Aida and Ace is my man. He's also the father of my baby."

Saadri was livid now. To come home from school and be faced with the ghetto behavior confronting her was more than she could take. They wanted a show but they would not get one from her. She looked at Aida and instantly knew the girl was as ignorant as her counterparts in the neighborhood. Aida stood in front of Saadri with hands on her hips, lips glowing from too much Vaseline, forehead shining with whatever concoction she used to slick down her 'baby hair'. Gold jewelry dripped from her ears, neck, wrists and fingers. She was the poster child for ghetto life. Saadri found her appearance laughable and had to stifle the urge to chuckle aloud. She had no intention of fighting the comical character before her; that made no sense. Instead she drew a quick, calming breath and arched her head a little higher. Through her periphery she saw Gary Stratton's smirk. The yard was silent with nervous anticipation; the event was worth a couple of weeks' gossip.

Again Saadri decided she would not give in to base behavior. She addressed Aida calmly. "Listen, I don't know what you've been told. What you and Najid do is your business. Leave me out of it and leave me alone." Saadri stepped away from Aida and attempted to enter the apartment building in which she lived for the third time.

When she realized Saadri wasn't going to create a scene, Aida yelled out, "I'd better not catch you with my man heifer, that's all I got to say!" She then stepped menacingly toward Saadri and extended her hand to strike, determined to provide a show of bravado.

Saadri spun toward Aida, caught her hand and almost threw her to the ground. Anger flared within her yet Saadri stayed mindful of not supplying the day's entertainment. "I already told you not to be in my face with this silliness!" Saadri dropped her book bag for balance and readied herself for Aida's counterattack when she was grabbed from behind. She put to good use skills from the self-defense classes she completed; she stomped the person's foot that grabbed her and spun in the opposite direction, still holding Aida's arm. Aida screamed in pain.

Rasheen held up his hands, "Saadri! Hold up! Stop girl! This is not you." Rasheen stepped between the embattled young women. Aida winced in pain as she began to explain herself to him. Rasheen wore a look of disgust that angered Saadri further. Saadri turned her back to Rasheen and Aida; she doubted the girl would come back for a second helping. The look on her face must have communicated there would be hell to pay; the porch dwellers fled as she stomped toward the entrance. Saadri ignored Rasheen's calls and entered her first floor apartment.

Ellen called out from her bedroom, "Hey baby! How was school today? Tell me what you did."

Saadri sighed and placed her bag in its usual corner near the kitchen table. She walked to the entrance of her mother's bedroom. "The day was good and in Black History we got into a deep discussion about DuBois and his 'crabs in a barrel' statement. I totally agree with the man after what I just went through to get in the front door."

Ellen's brows creased with concern, "What happened Saadri?"

Saadri relayed the events and fought to maintain her composure. The last thing she needed was to show her mother how deeply the incident affected her. Saadri awaited Ellen's response after she finished the story.

"Saadri."

The tone of her mother's voice grated on her already frayed nerves. Saadri spoke, "Mon mom, okay. You were right and I was wrong. What do you want me to say?"

Ellen sighed, "Is this what you want? Because this is all there is. That boy has been out there in those streets, you haven't and you are fooling yourself to think he is some Prince Charming. There's something unsettling about him Saadri, I told you that before and I'm not even talking about that girl. He won't stand for things to go any other way but the way he wants them to go. He wants complete control over everything and everyone. That includes you. If he hasn't shown that side to you yet, he will. Just leave him alone Saadri he's no good for you. Wall Street and Baruch my foot! He probably lied about all that and even if he didn't, he still has his head in the street." Ellen stopped and turned over to rest, she said enough. Saadri had to make up her own mind about Najid and the life he led.

Saadri went about her nightly routine of studying, making dinner, and reading. The phone rang at eight and Saadri's stomach fluttered. She reached the kitchen to answer the phone's third ring. "Hello."

"Candy! Hey baby! I was thinking about you today. I need some time with you. What's up?"

Saadri swallowed and said what she knew would not make Najid happy. "I don't have any time now or anymore for you. You take it easy Najid." She hung up the phone and exhaled a breath she wasn't aware she held. Her mother would be happy but Saadri felt her heart ache.

Chapter 4

The feeling had no time to take root because within ten minutes a more than perturbed Najid was on the other side of the door staring at her peephole. She debated whether to open the door, but thought it better to confront him in the privacy of her apartment. He stepped in before she could fully open the door.

"Would you mind explaining to me what that phone call was all about?!" His voice was low and demanding. Najid's orbs looked as if tempests were developing.

Saadri felt her resolve dwindle beneath his questioning gaze. She swallowed to regain composure and answered, "I said what I needed to say to you over the phone."

"Saadri don't play me for some chump cause you know I ain't! What has you flipping the script on me like this?!" Najid stepped further into the apartment and stood near as she locked the door.

She turned and bumped into him, Saadri knew the lines of power were laid out at that moment. How she responded determined whether she'd be a winner or not. When Najid edged closer and used her proper name again, "Saadri." she knew her battle was lost. There was no way she'd challenge him and cause confusion in her mother's house.

"Didn't your brother tell you?"

Najid sighed in exasperation, "I haven't seen Rah and I'm asking you. What is the problem? I call you after a long day of work, want to chill a little while with my lady and I get you going nut on the phone. Telling me to take it easy. You got me confused with those suckers you play around with up at that high school of yours. Now tell me what is on your mind and come straight cause my patience is worn thin. I can't believe you tried to play me like that!"

Saadri moved but Najid stood rooted as he waited for a response. She looked up at him with pleading eyes. "Can we sit down Najid?" He nodded and they settled on the couch with him close, an arm around her shoulder. "I was approached by a girl named Aida who said she had your baby and she took a swing at me before I could walk away from her. I would have broken her arm if Rah-Rah had not stopped me. After that I came in the building."

Najid watched her for a few moments before answering. He vacillated between stunned and explosive anger. Yet, his demeanor and facial expression remained calm. "Did you talk to Rah about the situation?"

"No, I was too upset. I came in the building and talked to my mother."

Najid squinted, "Why upset your mother with that stuff?"

Saadri's large eyes widened, "Because it was upsetting and she's my mother, that's why!"

Najid leaned close to her, "Wait a minute baby, I know you are upset but don't disrespect me. I'm concerned your mother is already sick and worrying her with nonsense like this isn't wise. Why couldn't you tell me this on the phone?"

Saadri was incensed, "I always talk to my mother and nothing changes that. After the double team I had, I didn't want to go through the explanation again."

Najid took hold of Saadri's shoulders, "What double team?!"

Saadri sucked a small bit of air. "First Gary got in my face about acting like I was too good and then being with you like you were so much of a better choice. Then that mess with Aida happened no sooner than I finally got away from Gary. It doesn't matter now because we are no longer together. Just leave it alone Najid, you and Aida can raise your baby and leave me alone. I don't need or want a bunch of drama."

Najid placed a hand beneath Saadri's chin and established an eye contact she dared not break. "For one thing, I have you and no one is going to take you away from me. Next, you have to be smart enough to realize everything isn't always what it seems. We are living here in this building and there are people who don't want us together but we have to be smart enough to see through that. You got played this afternoon and you have to be smarter than that."

Saadri retorted, "I am not in this street life."

Najid came back with, "You don't have to be but you still need to know how to handle it. It's not fair for you to let that craziness bring us drama because you can't peep game when you see it. You were set up so your response towards us would happen. This is your first and only one Saadri because I'm making sure of it. We don't need this. Let's step out a minute; get your jacket and keys. Tell your moms we won't be gone long, about an hour and a half." Najid released her and walked over to the door and waited for her to follow his directives.

Saadri finally saw the controlling nature as Najid expected complete compliance. She opened her mouth to speak but her throat went dry, Najid folded his arms across his broad chest and nodded at her. A feeling of déjà vu caused her to flash back to the time of David and Trinette's argument. She understood that nod perfectly, just like the others who'd fallen into the web Najid so masterfully wove.

A tiny part of her wanted to refuse to conform, wanted to see how he would handle an unexpected reaction. She watched him and saw the fleeting emotion just beneath his steely surface. He seemed genuinely disturbed and hurt by her actions. Saadri thought of her mother resting in the room and knew an argument between them would disturb her. She walked to her mother's bedroom and said she was going out for about an hour and a half. Ellen nodded, Saadri could tell she was feeling weaker and remembered it was one of her dialysis days. She gathered her keys and jacket. Najid opened the front door and they left quietly holding hands moving through the lobby.

Not that she expected anything different; the same people present in the yard during the earlier incident were also in the yard when Saadri and Najid appeared in the building's entrance.

Rasheen stood on the stoop with their crew, "Hey Saadri! You feeling better?"

Saadri shook her head, "Yeah Rah-Rah, a little." She nodded toward the others.

Najid looked at his brother, "Walk with us Rah." Najid wrapped his arm around Saadri's shoulder and held her protectively. He visually communicated with his crew; they were alert. The threesome dismounted the stoop and walked through the yard amidst a flurry of whispers. Najid wanted to clear the yard but Saadri was with him. He had a good idea of who engineered the day's episode and decided to do some fact-finding to confirm his suspicions. They continued through the yard and came to a bank of seats in a large playground area behind the building known as 'the circle'. The threesome found a vacant bench and settled in as Rasheen recounted what he knew of the incident. Najid listened intently, compared both stories and formulated a plan of action.

A short period of silence elapsed before he spoke. "You know my lady was ready to leave me over this Rah?"

Rasheen looked at his brother's face and knew someone would answer for the obvious stress Saadri's reaction caused. He felt compelled to defend her actions; he knew his brother could be hardened, "Put yourself in her shoes Ace. She comes home in a good frame of mind and gets hit with a bunch of drama over the guy she just got used to being her man. This is all new for her. You're still together right?"

Najid smirked, "You know it, but I can't let pettiness cause problems between us. Rah you know, I can't go through no more of this drama." Saadri shifted and Najid pulled her closer.

She scowled, "Why are you sitting here talking like I'm not even here?"

Najid's smile disappeared and Rasheen excused himself, "You two don't need me to be a third wheel." As he walked away he thought about the couple engaged in a face-off on the bench. Saadri had yet to truly understand the depth of his brother's personality and Najid had yet to learn how to deal with Saadri's strength. Their chemistry was either going to create a solid relationship or an explosion of incompatible personalities. The bottom line was - Saadri and Najid had both met their match.

Najid spoke slowly as he pulled Saadri closer, "There's a time and place for everything. You have to learn that."

Saadri felt her adrenaline speed up and she knew the things on her mind had to be voiced before she lost herself in dealing with the obviously angry Najid. "I feel like I'm one of your pawns Najid and that's not acceptable for me. I can't worry about what I say and wonder if I have done the right thing. I am supposed to be comfortable with you."

"I want you to feel comfortable Candy but I want your respect. You don't give me the benefit of the doubt and you shouldn't try to chump my face in front of other people, especially my brother."

Saadri defended, "That's not what I was trying to do."

Najid answered, "That's what you did."

Saadri sighed, "You're so tough sometimes I-"

Najid gathered her face within both hands and gave her a direct gaze, "What do you want Candy, a man that can protect and provide for you or a chump?"

"Of course I want a man, but I want to give something too."

Najid kissed her solidly on the lips, "Love me then, support me with your attention, your trust, your respect, and your cooperation. That's what I want and in return you'll have everything you need and want. Fair enough?"

"Fair enough, but I do have a mind and I want to be able to talk to you and say what I feel, you know. It's not disrespect because I do respect you, I need to be able to discourse with you, it's important to me."

Najid smiled, "Keep using words like that and we can talk all you want. I like having a smart girl who doesn't mind being a lady. Now that we have that squashed, I need some attention girl. You hung up on me, walked away from me, and tried to leave me tonight. I think you have a lot of making up to do for all you've put me through. Come here."

Saadri watched the approach of Najid's lips and she smiled. He was a wonderful kisser, not that she had much practice. Their mouths met and joined in a slow sensuous dance. Saadri relaxed and enjoyed their expression of caring. After a few moments, Najid intensified the kiss and Saadri began to wonder how long he'd be satisfied with only kissing her. When they ended the kiss, Najid smiled a lopsided grin, "You're getting sweeter Candy."

She laughed and lowered her head, embarrassed a bit. When she returned his gaze there was a question in her eyes.

"What's up baby?"

"I need to know if what that girl said was true Najid."

Najid took one of Saadri's hands and kissed it. "I met Aida over a year and a half ago out in Bushwick. She was the one time I went against my better judgment and I am paying for it. Truth is, she doesn't know who her daughter's father is and I'm being blamed. She's a cute little girl but I know she's not mine. We're scheduled to go to the lab next month for a blood test. I hate to do it but I need to know the truth. Besides, I was protected and… well, anyway. That's the deal Candy, but, rest assured, no one is coming in your face again."

Saadri questioned, "You're not going to do anything violent are you?"

Najid laughed, "Come on Candy, you should know me better than that. I will handle things like a man. Violence is not in my mind. So…"

Saadri looked at Najid's puckered lips and did not disappoint him.

With the height of football season upon them, cheerleading practice ran longer and more intense than normal. The girls sweated as the coach and captains demanded repetition of several technical drills. Precision was important for them to maintain early if they were going to win the state competition again in the spring. Saadri was more than happy with her front row position. She was asked to co-captain the team but refused because she knew she needed the flexibility to care for her mother. She thought about her mother as she executed the steps and cheers with the accuracy of a three-year veteran.

Ellen became adamant that Saadri continue with cheering once her illness progressed. Saadri smiled, her mother was a role model of courage and strength, and she hoped she could be half the woman her mother was.

Several members of the basketball team entered the gym and appreciatively admired the coordinated, attractive, and polished group of cheerleaders. Saadri, although elated for the end of practice, dreaded going home. Home meant Najid who she didn't particularly want to be around. Following a few more technical moves, the ladies finished and headed toward the bleachers to gather their belongings. The basketball team took over the floor to warm up.

She thought about the story Najid told her during her ride home …. Aida and Najid dated a few times. Najid thought she was someone he could get into until he realized that she was just a slightly tamer version of the money-grubbing, disreputable girls who were in too great a number in their neighborhood. They ended up parting ways and Najid was happy to be without her company for three months before she reappeared and announced she was carrying his child. Najid claimed he'd worn protection and didn't believe he fathered her child. Aida had agreed to get a blood test once the child was born. He thought they also agreed they weren't getting back together and would live their own lives. The issue was not resolved because Aida refused to get the baby tested. Najid took matters into his own hands and hired a lawyer through his job. The court appointed lab date approached in December.

Saadri felt tears welling up in her eyes but willed them not to fall. More than anything, she wanted to believe Najid, but the possibility that it could all be a lie stayed in her mind. She was not ready for the drama street life brought and wished she never agreed to that first date. Her reality had been turned upside down since Najid's entrance. If she tried to leave him alone, he would become upset and hound her until she talked to him. Then he would calm her fears and she would fall right back into the disconcerting cycle. The power Najid had over her scared Saadri because she knew she loved him.

Lost in her thoughts, Saadri didn't see Angelina Diaz approach her. "Earth to Saadri! What's wrong with you, Ace has your nose that open?"

Saadri looked at Angelina with a bright smile. She welcomed the distraction. "Long time no see Angie. What have you been up to? How is Chianna doing?"

Angelina laughed, "Of course it's long time no see. Ace hogs up your time. I'm good and my sister is as big as a house. She can't be having just one baby. Eric is sweating bullets, it's funny." They laughed together before Angelina continued. "Did you hear about Gary Stratton?!"

Saadri's stomach knotted with dread over the story to unfold. "No."

Angelina set in, "He messed with the wrong person. He was over in the Langston Hughes houses and some guys beat him up pretty bad. The guys stomped him out in front of one of the buildings. No one even tried to help him and the ones he was with left him on his own."

Saadri felt nauseated, "Who is responsible?" Angelina hesitated. Saadri spoke in a low, frightened voice. "Who are they saying is responsible? You can't tell me there is no word on the street because the story is out. Who had it done?"

Angelina looked at her friend as if she were seeing her for the first time. "You don't want to know that Saadri. I thought you knew about Gary. I'm sorry I even brought this up."

Saadri shook her head. Anger replaced her nausea. "I already have my answer." She walked on without saying goodbye. Angelina watched Saadri. Her friend had changed and she didn't think it was for the better.

Chapter 5

"Four hundred shares of Bilco Sports!" Najid held his pad in the air as he bellowed toward the processor. A quick nod let him know he fulfilled his order.

"Market is now closed for trading!!!" A collective round of disappointed sighs filled the air as runners began to clear the trading floor. Najid left with a grin, the day was hectic but productive.

The grandfatherly gentleman, who watched with pride, approached him. "You've done well today son. Are you ready to step it up?"

Najid nodded, "I'm ready to soak in all you're willing to teach me Mr. Grey, and then some."

Edwin Grey laughed aloud, "I like that edge you have Najid. Then some... Always make sure you have the 'then some'." Edwin demonstrated pride in his protégé. He met Najid over three years earlier when he was a mailroom clerk. The street smart, tough young man had a grit Edwin could identify with. Upon further conversation he realized Najid had a great deal of intelligence. Edwin began grooming him since that time.

Now Najid was a runner on the floor of 'the market' and he was good. He demonstrated tenacity men twice his age would have paid millions for. Edwin Grey had plans for Najid. The two walked off the floor discussing the upcoming training that would take Najid from runner to processor.

Najid walked through the streets of lower Manhattan to gather innumerable thoughts flowing through his head. He never fought the craziness of the subway ride home without the cleansing ritual. As he walked he passed a jewelry store and stopped to browse the window. A white gold herringbone necklace and earring set caught his attention. Najid pictured the set adorning Saadri's caramel skin. He determined she would look good in the pieces and they would cheer her up. She still wasn't too happy about the situation with Aida; ever since he explained it to her she had been distant. Without hesitation he walked into the store to make the purchase, his lady deserved the best.

Saadri walked into the quiet apartment after ten. She didn't bother turning on many lights as she headed to her mother's room. Ellen needed a few things to make her hospital stay more comfortable. Palpitations from a weakened heart caused her to be admitted for tests. Saadri prayed all would be well and they would find her mother a new kidney. A soft knock on the door stopped her from completely packing the bag sitting on her mother's bed. She answered it and in a matter of moments Najid's commanding presence filled the living room.

Najid was so glad to see Saadri he failed to notice the worn expression on her face. The lights were off as he waited for her to secure the door. Immediately, he enfolded her in his arms, "Hey baby. I missed you today." His lips came down on hers and she didn't disappoint him. When he finally came up for air, Saadri moved away and turned on a lamp. Najid sucked in a breath when he saw her face.

"What's wrong baby?" Najid pulled Saadri into his embrace again.

Saadri laid her head against his chest and sighed, "I'm just tired. My mother went to the hospital and they're keeping her for tests. Her heart is weak and her kidneys are getting worse. I keep praying cause I know God can heal her, it's just hard to see her like this."

Najid held on as he marveled at the strength of the young woman who came to mean more to him than she knew. "It takes a lot of guts to be able to go through what you go through and still maintain a positive attitude."

Saadri looked up at him, "It's called faith Najid."
The twosome settled onto the couch where Najid held Saadri in his lap. Her head nestled in the crook of his shoulder as he massaged her arm and hair. Occasionally he kissed her forehead but they said little.

"Do you need me to stay with you tonight?"

Saadri sat up quickly and left Najid's lap, she headed toward the kitchen. "Non. That won't be necessary."

Najid frowned, "It's not about necessity and even if it were, it's okay for you to need me. I am your man." He moved toward the kitchen.

Saadri puttered around the kitchen, "Yeah I know. But, I'm cool."

Najid stood in the kitchen's entrance and folded his arms across his chest. "Why do you do this Saadri?"

She turned nervously toward him as she heard her proper name, "Do what?"

He removed his arms and rested them on his waist, "You withdraw and act like I can't do anything for you."

Saadri retorted, "What do you want? For me to be a sniveling little baby?"

"No, that's not the lady I asked out."

"I don't think you know who you asked out. You have this picture in your head of who I'm supposed to be and you don't see anything else." Saadri walked into her mother's bedroom and finished packing the bag. She was at wits end, too much happened and too many people demanded of her. Enough was enough.

Najid followed her with furrowed brows, "Don't tell me who I-"

She rounded on him. "Stop thinking you can order me around like I'm one of your henchmen! You don't know me like you think you do! I can think for myself and I don't like playing follow the leader!"

Najid bit out, "Oh, you're so liberated you don't need a man to do nothing for you! You better watch yourself before you find yourself, by yourself!"

"I was born and will die by myself, so that's no big thing!" Saadri yelled at Najid.

He stood stock-still and glared at her. "Tell me straight up Saadri. If you don't want me around then say so. I've been busting my butt for over five months now trying to show you it's all about you and you have given me your backside to kiss the whole way. So you tell me now, as much as I want you, I will leave you alone. Just say the word."

Saadri sneered, "Don't act like it's all about me! You think I don't know about what happened over in Langston Hughes?! The girls in your face from Van Dyke and out in East New York and the ones in Bed Stuy! Miss Goody Two Shoes is supposed to be stupid!? You're waiting on blood tests for one kid and probably have a million more out there somewhere and you expect me to act like a little wife to you. You're just like the rest of these thugs out here, only you're the King Thug."

Najid received his answer, "The King Thug? That's what you think of me?" Saadri folded her arms and walked into her bedroom. She flopped on her bed; Najid followed her and sat on the far end. "Look, the only reason I'm even sitting here right now is because I know you have been through a lot. I can't begin to imagine what you feel or go through with your mother being so sick and your father being gone.

Anyway, I know you hear a lot through the grapevine out there but I told you before you have to be smarter than to believe everything you hear. However, I am not about to sit here and pay for your misconceptions. The whole time we've been together that's what I've been doing and I can't do that anymore. I'm running after you, looking for you, calling you, tracking you down, and seeing about you. None of this time have you done that for me, I don't even get the benefit of the doubt from you. If I did, we wouldn't be sitting here engaged in this conversation. It's like you hold me at a distance and I have to prove I'm for real with you."

Saadri sat up and looked at Najid, "I-"

Najid held his hand up. "Don't. Listen, I was not responsible for Langston Hughes – I know you're talking about Gary. He was messing around with some drug dealers from Harlem and they caught up to him."

Saadri was about to speak but Najid continued. "I'm not doing this anymore; you need to figure out if you really want me so we won't waste each other's time. I'll give you your space. I won't be calling or coming by or tracking you down. The next move is on you. As for these females you're talking about, there is no one more important to me than you." He rose and prepared to leave. "My last order, as you put it, is to come and lock the door."

The two walked silently to the door. Saadri kept a steady pace behind him. Her mouth felt like it held a ball of cotton. She wanted to stop him but had no response to the truth he told. She made him pay for her failure to deal effectively with the negative press involved in their being together. Not once over the five months had she uttered an endearing word of her own volition. Her responses were always prompted. She watched his muscular frame and knew she would miss him. Saadri sighed; it was best to end it before anyone experienced more pain.

Najid touched the doorknob, spun around and enfolded Saadri in his arms. His lips crushed hers, as they spoke what words couldn't express. Saadri matched his fervor and readied to ask for his forgiveness. Najid broke the kiss, "Like I said, I've always shown you how I feel. The next move is on you." He left with no further word.

Rasheen watched his brother walk into the room they shared. He knew something wasn't right in his body language. It had to be Saadri; they'd been going at it for the past several weeks. He spoke softly, "What's the verdict man?"

Najid let out a breath, "Not good. It's on her now. I'm tired of fighting for her acceptance. You know, I just found out tonight that I've been paying for her inability to deal with all this game out here. Ain't that a kick in the teeth?"

Rasheen laughed, "That must be something from Wall Street man! Give her time. Her mom's sick and in and out of the hospital all of the time… there's a lot of pressure on her. She probably doesn't know whether she's coming or going."

Najid threw up his hands, "Yeah, but I'm the one there, steady as a beat and I get kicked around like yesterday's garbage."

Rasheen advised, "Give her time to sort it all out. She has to see what she has. Unfortunately for her, it has to be after you're gone. She'll come around."

Najid ground out, "Well, she'd better man cause…"

Rasheen affirmed, "I already knew that man, I'm glad you know."

Saadri walked away from the door dazed. She leaned over to turn out the lamp when she saw a long rectangular box with a card attached. Saadri picked the items up and wondered when Najid had placed them on the lamp table. She opened the card and read:

Candy

> I'll give you the world. Just let me.

Najid

Her eyes misted as she opened the box. She retrieved the herringbone set and the misting burst forth into uncontrollable tears. Why did she let the man she loved walk out the door as she had?

Saadri stalled at least ten times before knocking on the Raenier's door. Margie Raenier opened shortly after, "Well, isn't this a pleasant surprise? Come on in honey." Saadri stepped into the impeccably maintained apartment and fought for composure. Margie's soft voice pulled her attention from her nerves. "Najid's not here. He is working later since he got the promotion." Saadri tried valiantly to hide her surprise and shame. Margie smiled, "I'm glad you're here. It gives us a chance to have a good talk. Let's sit on the couch."

The ladies sat and Margie began immediately. "I admire you Saadri. You carry yourself very well. That's why my son fell for you."

Saadri looked at the pattern of the couch. "Thank you Miss Margie."

"I know you two aren't together anymore. What Najid won't tell me, Rasheen will. I know what people say about my son and I don't make any excuses for him or Rasheen. Their father and I have raised them to understand that men must take care of themselves. Najid and

Rasheen have also learned they have to deal with the consequences of their actions. Najid has always been a strong willed, go-getter; it's what brought him so far on Wall Street. He didn't always go in the right direction but he definitely is now. I know some of that change is due to you."

"Miss Margie, I-"

Margie stopped her, "Listen Saadri, you have to do what makes you happy and that's not always what makes everyone else happy. Plenty of people didn't like Jack when I started with him, friends and family included. I loved Jack and he treated me well. I never regretted a day with him and I certainly don't regret having my boys. If you love Najid then he's the one you need to be with because you will be miserable if you aren't. Any other guy will be a substitute and that's where trouble can begin. We'll find out about the baby and if she is his then he will take care of her but he still loves you. Don't listen to all of the gossip going on around here; it's called gossip because it's designed to destroy. Go by the way Najid treats you and if he doesn't treat you the way you want to be treated then leave him alone, with no regrets."

Saadri didn't realize she was crying until she felt several streams of water flowing down her cheeks. "It's just so much. I didn't know what to do."

Margie placed a well-manicured hand under Saadri's chin. "Honey, when it all comes at you like this, you have to hold onto what has been real. If you blow a good thing do you know how many Nay Sayers will jump at the chance to get what you had? The same people who tell you all of that garbage about Najid would make him their man as soon as he gave the consent. Women are catty Saadri; they'll mess up what you have because nothing is going well in their lives. If you want that man you had better get him and keep him."

Saadri listened to Najid's mother and could see him clearly in her voice and mannerisms. She was cool personified and it was a comfort when Saadri needed it the most. It was good Najid was not in the apartment when she arrived. Then, she wouldn't have received the chance to become better acquainted with Margie Raenier.

"How is your mother doing? Is she home yet? Or when will she be coming home?"

Saadri smiled at the question and relaxed as she talked about her mother.

Ellen came home from the hospital two weeks later, but with physician's orders to hire a full-time nurse. Saadri called her father and Damas flew in to assist her with plans for Ellen's care. They were elated to secure the services of Mary Clark, a 'mother' in the church Ellen and Saadri attended regularly. Damas stayed two weeks, long enough to demonstrate his continued love for Ellen. Saadri particularly enjoyed the time Damas spent with her and Teran, her younger sister by another mother. He took them shopping and did all he could to keep up with their high school careers and college plans.

The two weeks her father remained in New York with them, helped Saadri avoid thinking about how she missed Najid. It was also easy to leave things as they were because Najid, as Rasheen informed her, worked long hours and was scheduled to resume classes in January for the spring semester. The time just did not seem right for reconciliation but Saadri hoped the opportunity would present itself before it was too late to do anything about the damage her distrust had caused.

Chapter 6

January 1983

Thursday afternoon, students met with guidance counselors to sign up for additional college testing, college fairs, and to pick up applications. Saadri decided against retaking the SAT since she knew she planned to stay local. She discussed plans for the future with her counselor and took two final exams. Afterward she met her younger sister Teran and some friends to celebrate her birthday which occurred earlier in the week. They went to the home of a classmate after picking up hero sandwiches and enjoyed each other's company until early in the evening. Saadri was glad Teran came with her but could tell Teran fought to remain jovial. She called their gathering to an end once Teran took a drink; they were headed back home by five. She was more than happy to meet the aroma of a freshly prepared meal when she walked through her door.

Mary Clark smiled at the young woman she watched grow from a small child. "How was school today?"

"It was busy Ma Mary. I had to take two tests and meet with the guidance counselor. I am kind of beat but I still have some studying to do."

Mary nodded appreciatively, "Good, it will keep you busy and out of trouble. Let me know when you're ready for your supper. I made some peach cobbler too. Go see your mama; she had a good day. Got up out of that bed a little and stretched those limbs. She's in good spirits."

Saadri placed her bag in its customary spot and thanked Mary before heading into her mother's bedroom. "Hey Mon mon! I heard you had a busy day walking and stretching. You didn't overdo it did you?"

Ellen smiled, "Hey Baby Girl. I'm about as well as can be expected. God is good and I won't complain. It was good to get up. You're home early today. Is everything okay at school? How did your meeting go with the guidance counselor, you did remember what I told you to tell them, didn't you?"

"Wi Mon mon, I won't be taking the SAT again and I paid for the application to CUNY. My counselor also told me I should also apply to places like New Paltz, St. John's, Fordham, Iona, and some of the other colleges that are still close to the city. I took the applications and thought I'd talk it over with you." Saadri pointed toward the book bag she laid near the dining table. She met Ellen's intense stare and averted her eyes.

Ellen spoke directly, "I haven't seen our boy around here lately, what's the deal?"

Saadri answered quickly, "You've been out of it so how would you know?"

Ellen smirked, "Now you know Ma Mary is my eyes and ears and she hasn't seen or heard of him. Now, tell me what's up."

"We aren't together anymore, that's what's up."

"You don't sound thrilled with that state of affairs." Ellen paid keen attention to her daughter's body language.

Saadri sighed, "I would think you'd be happy."

Ellen shook her head vehemently, "Oh no you don't! You are not going to put this on me. You accepted the date and the relationship because you wanted to. I told you I didn't particularly care for the idea but I can't say he's shown anything but the utmost respect for you. Even when he bossed you around."

Saadri turned toward Ellen with a ready protest, "Non –"

"Yes he did! He may not have yelled but he did. That boy has a serious control thing going on. So, why did you two break up?"

Saadri threw up her hands in resignation. "He said I didn't show him I was into the relationship like he was and that he wasn't going to chase me anymore. Najid said the next move was mine. That was when you were in the hospital."

Ellen shook her head, "And what exactly did he want from you as proof that you were into the relationship as he put it?"

Saadri laughed a little but answered quickly so as not to give Ellen the wrong impression. "He said I didn't call him or show him I really cared for him. I wasn't demonstrating I wanted him or the relationship. It wasn't about sex though because he knew up front that I didn't believe in doing anything before I was married."

Ellen sat up with Saadri's assistance. "Well? Was what Najid said true? If it was, you were unfair to him. Why did you start off with him anyway? There are plenty of boys in-"

This time Saadri interrupted. "Please don't start in on the church! You know good and well those boys in our church don't have a thing to offer anyone! Najid has more sense than all of them."

Ellen was perturbed, "They have Christ and that's way more than Najid has! You need to get off your high horse and get it together if you think you're going to find a husband!"

Saadri stood from her mother's bed, "I don't want any of them! All they have is Jesus and they are waiting on Jesus to do everything for them. They don't try to do anything for themselves!"

"Saadri Isaure Buard! You are not too good for a saved man! You need to get your attitude together! There's a youth fellowship tomorrow night, Ma Mary told me about it and you're going. It's time you get your head out of the streets where you found that boy and take a stand for the Lord. You can't serve two masters!"

Saadri felt tears threaten to overflow her orbs. She stood with her head raised to the ceiling trying to regain composure. She took a few calming breaths and spoke slowly, "I am not interested in going to the Youth Night."

Ellen ground out, "You will go and you will mind yourself. Get your sister to go with you; Lord knows she needs some Christian influence because she's not getting it from her Mama! I'm still the mother here, at least until I rest my head." She watched Saadri walk out of the room and instantly felt remorse over forcing her daughter to attend the event. The last thing Ellen wanted was to be the cause of Saadri rejecting the church. After things calmed down between them, she would make it a point of talking to her daughter. With her health teetering, Ellen felt an urgency to know Saadri's personal convictions and beliefs about salvation and living a saved lifestyle.

Saadri stalked out of her mother's room and into the hefty figure of Mary Clark. "Don't come out here all mad because your food won't taste right. And don't think about telling me you're not hungry because I slaved over this stove today whipping up all of your favorites - smothered chicken, mashed potatoes from scratch, onion gravy, collard greens, candied yams, and buttery cornbread. Don't forget I made that cobbler and if you don't eat dinner I'll see to it you won't have a bite!"

Saadri laughed, Ma Mary pretended to be tough but she was like the grandmother Saadri missed having. Her own grandmother died when she was six years old and her grandfather died shortly after she was born. She sat at the table and agreed to Mary's demands.

Mary saw the sadness sweep across Saadri's features and quelled the urge to gather the young woman in her arms. She knew Saadri to be a highly independent girl who didn't accept coddling. She also understood Saadri had to grow up fast to best deal with her mother's chronic illness. Mary continued to pray fervently for the young woman who had the world before her. She fixed a medium-portioned plate for the willowy eighteen-year old and set the food before her in a flourish of grandeur.

Saadri laughed, "Why thank you Madam."

Mary eased into a chair and smiled, "Why tis my pleasure Kind Miss. You have some mail from your daddy, your grandmamma, and your older sister. I also have a little something for you on your dresser."

"Thank you Miss Mary, I wasn't expecting anything from you. I will look at everything once I finish eating. This meal looks delicious." Saadri graced her food and began to make steady work of it.

Mary began a conversation. "I just want you to know I'm proud of the way you have grown up. You are quite a young woman. Eighteen is a big number but I know you will handle it well."

Saadri looked up, "Thank you for noticing Miss Mary." She then nodded toward her mother's bedroom. "Some people don't seem to realize that."

Mary gave a nonchalant wave, "Oh, well, some folk see things changing faster than they can control and it's frightening, that's all. You have a special young man you pining over?"

Saadri shook her head, "Not anymore. You probably wouldn't have liked him either."

Mary frowned, "What was not to like? Did your mama like him?"

Saadri shook her head and spoke between mouthfuls of food. "No. He was too into the streets for her but he didn't show me that side of him. I can only think of one occasion and after that nothing else happened. It's like he walks on both sides of the fence. First, he has a group he hangs out with, they're not a gang but they have a lot of clout. Then he works and goes to college. I know he doesn't take any nonsense from anyone but he has never mistreated me."

Mary questioned, "Why does it sound like you're trying to convince me? Then again, I think you're trying to convince yourself. This boy seems to have made his choice, are you going to let him pull you into his world?" Mary rose from the table. "Baby, I need to feed and tend your mama. You eat up and get your lessons out. Don't worry about the kitchen, I'll get it cleaned."

Saadri could not seem to get her sister Teran out of the funk she was in. Teran and her boyfriend Bashan were having problems and Teran was not one to handle setbacks well. Rather than bring her along and have her ruin the night for everyone, Saadri figured it best to leave her at home. As they ended their call Saadri promised to check on her after the event was over.

The youth night celebration took place at a neighborhood skating rink. Several area churches combined their efforts to provide a more positive outlet for the youth of their congregations. It surprised Saadri to see the excellent turnout and she quickly spotted five of the sixteen youth in the church she attended. Many more unrecognizable faces continuously circled the skating area as popular Christian music wafted from the speakers.

Saadri caught the eye of Cedric Sailor. He waved her over to the group. When she arrived, he began to tease. "Well, look what the wind blew in! To what do we owe this pleasure Lady Madonna?"

Saadri rolled her eyes and addressed the group. "Hey everybody. Miss Mary told me about tonight so I thought I'd come out. I missed the other three nights."

Mary's granddaughter Bethany spoke, "I'm glad you came out. I hear your mother is doing well."

Saadri nodded, "She's fine and hasn't changed a bit. Thanks for the concern."

Cedric interjected, "Are you going to ignore me all night or skate with me?"

Cedric stunted her acerbic comment when he took hold of Saadri's arm and led her to the skate rental counter. "I'm glad you came out tonight. We were beginning to think you didn't like our company. We'll have a ball, you'll see."

True to his words, the night was fun-filled. Saadri couldn't believe eleven thirty came as she walked to the counter to return her skates. Usually like oil and water, Saadri marveled at how well she and Cedric got along on this night. When she realized his amorous intentions, Saadri tactfully informed him she was not interested in a relationship and felt relieved when he graciously accepted her position.

As she sat on a bench tying her boots, Cedric seated himself beside her. "Hey friend, how are you getting home?"

Saadri smiled, "The same way I got here friend, the train."

Cedric nodded, "I figured as much. Do you know of anyone who's going your way?"

Saadri shook her head. "I figured that much too. You independent women live too dangerously. I'll get my brother and we'll see you home." Cedric raised his hand to cut off Saadri's protest. "Sometimes you have to let someone else do something for you Saadri. Let a man be a man, you know."

Saadri bit her lower lip, "I've been accused of that before. I'm sorry."

Cedric shrugged, "I guess he's the reason why I won't get a chance. Anyway, no apology necessary, I'll be back in a minute."

The threesome boarded the Number Three train at the Franklin Ave. station amidst a hail of laughter. Cedric teased his younger brother Eric about the number of times he fell in the rink. Saadri tried to mediate as best she could but Cedric's comic expressions caused her to scream with laughter. They found seats and calmed their conversation enough to begin discussing plans after high school.

Eric began, "I applied for the Morehouse's early entrance program and will hear something in February. If I'm accepted then I will leave in the middle of July. I've been fasting and praying for God to move on my behalf."

Cedric's sixteen-year old younger brother impressed Saadri. She also noticed how Cedric withdrew from the conversation. Curious, she questioned him, "Are you coming out of school in the spring too Cedric."

Cedric shook his head, "I came out two years ago. I'm just waiting on the Lord to give me some direction."

Saadri furrowed her brows. "What school do you attend?"

Cedric answered, "I don't right now. I'm trying to see which one the Lord wants me to attend."

Saadri felt her face heating with agitation. "Oh, so you're working while you wait."

Cedric shrugged his shoulders, "I'm between jobs right now."

Saadri could have screamed. This guy had the nerve to turn on the charm yet had nothing to offer. This was the very thing she tried to tell her mother. Saadri refocused on Eric again and spotted a familiar profile. She swallowed to calm her nerves. "So Eric, are you on any teams at school?"

Eric spoke quickly. He realized how bad his older brother looked in Saadri's eyes but was powerless to change the stigma Cedric created. "I only do baseball because I work part-time."

Saadri nodded and thought about how trifling Cedric was compared to Eric. She congratulated, "I think you have it quite together and I think Morehouse would be crazy not to accept you early." She and Eric settled into easy conversation in spite of a brooding Cedric.

Chapter 7

They disembarked the train at the Rockaway Ave. station and took approximately three steps. "Saadri."

She turned toward Najid on unsteady legs. "Hi Najid."

Najid nodded toward the brothers as he strolled toward Saadri, "You're getting home kind of late, were you out celebrating your birthday?"

Saadri exhaled a calming breath, "I went to a skating party sponsored by the youth ministry tonight down at Empire."

Najid nodded, "So you're on your way to the building now?"

Saadri concurred, "Yes. Uh, Najid, this is Eric and Cedric. They rode with me."

Najid looked at the two young men and raised his head, "What's up?"

While Eric extended Najid the greeting of the day, he turned to Saadri, "Why didn't you remind us it was your birthday? We'll make this up to you." Cedric nodded; Najid gave him a once over that didn't escape Saadri's notice.

Saadri decided to deescalate the mounting tension. She moved toward the steps, the guys followed, and spoke aloud. "Thank you guys for escorting me. Najid and I live in the same building so you won't have to leave the train station."

Eric nodded in agreement and gave Saadri a brotherly hug at the bottom of the steps. Cedric mumbled, "Later," and walked by her toward the southbound platform.

Saadri watched the two quicken their pace in an effort to catch a train that pulled into the track overhead. Najid spoke in her ear, "Have you watched Lover Boy long enough?"

She turned toward him and realized how much she missed Najid being around. He stood before her, handsome as ever, with a coordinating burgundy Kangol hat perched low over his brow. "Hello yourself Najid, he's not my boyfriend."

"Yeah, but he wants to be." Najid walked ahead of her and held open the gate for them to leave the waiting area. They descended the stairs side by side.

Saadri was secretly happy he responded jealously, she answered, "Yeah, but he can't be."

Najid stopped them on the first landing leading them to the street below. The chill in the air escaped their notice. "Why is that?"

Saadri looked boldly in his eye, "Because I'm not over you. I have missed you these past two months. Plus I never had the chance to either return your gift or to thank you for it."

Najid continued walking down the stairs. "Is that right?"

Saadri walked beside him and slipped her gloved hand into his. "Yes, that's right. You were right about a lot of things. I want things to be different this time."

Najid tightened his grip on her hand and turned her to face him, "What makes you think you're not too late? Two months is a long time."

Saadri spoke softly, "She hasn't had time to love you. I do."

Najid stood stock-still. His dark eyes deadpanned, "Don't say things you don't mean."

Saadri stepped within mere inches of his face, "I love you Najid and I'm sorry for hurting you."

Najid shifted slightly, "Who said I was hurt? I was pissed; I don't like my time being wasted."

Saadri saw through his façade, "I love you Najid and I'm sorry. Those guys go to my church and we are friends."

Najid shook his head, "What am I supposed to do with you Candy?"

Saadri stood on the toes of her boots, "Well, for starters, forgive me." She wrapped her arms around Najid's neck and wasn't disappointed when he hugged her as tightly as possible, their heavy winter coats created a barrier. His kiss let her know she was forgiven.

He held her long enough to steady his erratic heartbeat, then spoke, "Let's get home before we freeze out here. Your nose is red and I can feel my toes tingling." They walked toward Tilden housing as Najid spoke, "So that dude was trying to push up on you wasn't he?"

Saadri looked at him a moment before answering, "He showed a few signs but I told him I wasn't looking for that kind of involvement with him. He took it all in stride. I was there to enjoy myself and I ended up having a pretty good time. Maybe you could come to one with me."

Najid shook his head, "I don't know. I never was big on church. Everyone is so phony."

Saadri was insulted, "I'm in church Najid, have I been phony too?"

He answered firmly, "No and that's another thing that makes you so different. However, the rest of the folks are another story. I have seen that dude around and he wasn't talking about God. Now I suppose he's acceptable to your mother, isn't he? All because when he runs his game he brings it into the church. It's still game and that's why so many dudes are able to get over in these churches."

Saadri tried to interject but Najid continued, "I admit, I have not been good all my life but I have not been afraid to work for what I get. These past two months without you really had me thinking hard. I was thinking before that, but after we split, I really started thinking and making some changes. I know there are some things about me you can't deal with and you shouldn't have to. Those things are no longer a factor. I go to work, go through my training, and most times I am not hitting the block until after ten thirty. Tonight I stopped off and got a bite with some classmates. Training ended so now I get back into the books at Baruch."

Saadri watched Najid with an expression of respect and glee. "I know you want things out of life Candy and I intend to go after those things with you. If this night never happened, believe me, I would have been on your door within the month. Truth be told, I love you too."

"Yes!" Saadri wrapped her arms around Najid's neck and kissed him soundly.

When they broke Najid laughed. "Girl, you can get a little crazy can't you? Let's hurry up and get to the building. It's cold out here." He gathered her close to his side as they quickened the pace.

Saadri entered the church as she normally did, the day before service, in order to pray and help where she could. Things at home were not as peaceful as they could be since Ellen strongly dissented of Saadri's decision to start dating Najid again. Even Miss Mary came against her decision stating that she was unequally yoked with Najid. Miss Mary also stated that Najid not being saved made him unsuitable even for consideration as a mate. Saadri was livid; she loved Najid and began to understand some of his reasoning for not attending church. They'd even gone so far as to tell her that Cedric needed a good woman like her to bring him along. She challenged with Cedric not having anything compared to Najid. When they countered with Cedric being in the church as making him suitable the hypocrisy was almost too much for her.

As she approached the front of the church, the pastor's voice rang out. "Sister Saadri! I would like to talk to you in my office."

The sudden command startled Saadri. She retraced her steps and walked quietly to the pastor's office. Once inside she waited no more than a few minutes before the most unnerving conversation of her life began.

"Saadri, I understand you have taken up with one of the neighborhood thugs. You have been taught better than to lower your standards like this. I would like to begin some counseling sessions with you to get at what's really bothering you. It would break my heart to have you sitting in front of me pregnant out of wedlock."

Saadri felt lightheaded; she formed her words carefully. "Pastor Kent I am not involved with a neighborhood thug. My boyfriend works a full-time job and goes to training classes on his job and college classes at night. We have never been intimate; he has respected my wishes to wait until marriage. When we're together we talk about things going on around the neighborhood, various leaders, many academic topics, and us. He's one of the most intelligent men I know. As for his past, we have all gotten into things we are not proud of. He's a changed young man and I enjoy being around him very much."

Pastor Kent answered, "Do you really care for him or are you rebelling against your mother?"

She sucked in a breath, "Pastor, my mother and I have our share of issues but we also know she has fragile health. Knowing this, we don't engage in drawn out tug-of-war. No Sir, I am not rebelling, neither of us have time for that. Sure, we have our share of disagreements, but life for us is too limited to hold grudges or get into power matches. No, I am not with him out of rebellion against my mom."

Pastor Kent leaned forward, "Then you need to stop grieving your mother with this relationship you're having."

Saadri was livid but said nothing. She knew Ellen to be bold and forthright as she expressed her opinion on many occasions. However, it was hard for Saadri to understand why her mother would speak to the pastor about being grieved over her and Najid's relationship. Unhappy about a decision was one thing but being grieved was another. Saadri spoke with the pastor a total of a half-hour. She left the office full of questions, something wasn't adding up.

"Sorry it had to go down that way but I knew you wouldn't have taken it well from me."

Saadri looked at Cedric with ire. "So, you're the reason I've been pulled into the office. You have a lot of nerve."

Cedric lifted his hands in an innocent gesture. "I was just looking out for you as your brother in Christ. That dude is-"

Saadri pointed an angry finger at his chest, "That dude as you call him is none of your business! However, since you're looking out for my best interests as a brother in Christ then I'll do the same for you. That dude has more going for him than you have the gumption to get. While you're sitting back waiting for some sign to drop from the sky he is out there working and going to school. That's why we can't get people in the church, because the ones in here are always hiding their laziness behind Jesus and people out there have more than the ones who proclaim to serve a mighty God!"

Cedric spat, "That dude is after one thing and you think you have it all together but he'll trip you up! You don't even know what that guy is about or what he has done! You young girls are so naïve; the street guys get you every time. I thought you would have been different, you want a thug instead of a brother who loves the Lord and will treat you like something!"

Saadri raised her voice, "You don't even have anything to offer! You don't have a job, not trying to find one, and no post-high school education! What reason would I have to be with you and not my boyfriend who has more than two dimes to rub together? You're supposed to be so much better because you're in this church? This church is all you have and that won't pay any bills. While you wait for God to tell you what your younger brother has sense enough to do, I'll be with a young man who respects me, what I stand for and who isn't afraid to go out and be a man!"

Cedric sneered, "It won't last and you'll end up pregnant! Then you'll want to come crawling back to me!"

Saadri readied her reply but stopped as the pastor appeared in the hall outside his office; his expression was one of great disdain. Saadri looked at her pastor, Cedric's father, and spoke evenly, "I thank you for speaking with me Pastor, although I have to admit the source's motives need to be questioned."

Pastor Kent Sailor spoke, "I've certainly gained new information to consider Saadri. We'll talk more at a later time; I still have concerns. You should be getting back home; I don't want you traveling too late. Tell your mother I'll call her during the day tomorrow." He then looked at his second oldest son. "Cedric, come on in here so I can talk to you."

Mary lugged the heavy cart onto the porch and easily opened the metal entrance door. She thought of Saadri and wondered how long it would be before she arrived home from the church. Before Saadri left, Mary and her granddaughter Bethany came to watch over Ellen. They heard the two trading angry words. Mary hoped to speak with Ellen before Saadri came back. As she pondered relations between the two women, Mary's thoughts were interrupted by a figure in her periphery. A young man dressed in the latest fashion stared directly at her. The stare unnerved Mary, the young man knew she checked him out and did nothing to conceal the fact that he, too, gave her a thorough perusal. When he spoke Mary jumped from the strength of his voice.

"That cart is pretty loaded. May I help you to your door?"

Mary returned, "How do you know where my door is?"

The young man tilted his chin, "I don't, but the way you're facing makes me think you're just going up to the first floor. Would you like some help? I wouldn't want you to hurt your back or anything like that."

Mary instantly disliked the young man's self-assured mien. "I'll manage just fine. Have a good night."

The young man lifted his hands in a questioning gesture, "Are you sure? You'll be okay?"

Mary watched him a second and thought of a term to describe him; he was a smooth operator. In her mind he was also trouble. "I will be fine young man. You can go on along." Mary observed the young man as he looked at his watch and turn toward the exit. He departed with a tip of his head. Mary got the groceries into the house and Bethany helped her put them away.

Chapter 8

Few people knew of Najid's predictive ability. His brother used to call him a warlock but he stopped him. He didn't like the stigma that went along with the title. Najid knew his ability gave him a competitive edge in anything he undertook. It was easy to fall into the cycle of events involved with street life. His father told him everyone was looking for someone to follow but that everyone could not lead. Najid realized early, he possessed that special ability to lead; others sensed it and naturally looked to him to know the answers. His intuitive sense helped him to know how to lead them.

His father also taught him leaders needed to be sharp, well-learned, and cautious. Najid learned these lessons and groomed himself into a respected persona in East New York. Although, there was one lesson his father taught that he'd not heeded - the love of a good woman can turn any man around. Saadri broadsided Najid; he wasn't prepared to feel for her as intensely as he did. The love he felt changed his perspective. Najid had a plan; he knew where he wanted to go in life, every step of the way. He planned to use the streets as a means to a better end. When he found himself caring more about a future with Saadri Buard those plans abruptly curbed.

Saadri was a lady who had hopes and deserved better than what Brownsville could offer. Najid changed his lifestyle and settled in for the hardest battle he ever fought - winning Saadri as his mate. Once outside the building, Najid intended to go up to a corner store, purchase munchies and head to Eric Eason's apartment. Chianna Diaz had two boys who were two months old. Najid wanted to give them something for the boys. He thought about the couple living in Eric's apartment, Eric's parents moved back to Georgia. Najid knew he wanted to be with Saadri like that – every day.

He crossed Rockaway Ave. and looked down the street out of habit. The train station beckoned so Najid crossed over Blake Ave. and walked in its direction. On his way, he stopped in a store, bought a snack, soda and a paper, and walked on. The closer he came to the station the clearer his mind became on why he was there - he was waiting for Saadri. A slight smile on his face, he walked on. A little ways up he saw her, "Candy!"

The young lady turned toward Dumont Avenue and Najid frowned, "Candy!" She continued walking and Najid was sure he yelled her name loud enough. When he caught up to her he was more than perturbed. He gently stopped her stride in the middle of the block. "Where are you going in such a hurry that you couldn't acknowledge I called you Saadri?"

"I'm not Saadri but you must be her boyfriend Najid. Hi. I'm Teran, Saadri's sister." The young woman smiled.

Najid stood a moment. "What's with the games Candy?"

Teran laughed and placed a hand on her hip. "I just told you I am not my sister. You really can't tell the difference?" She shook her head and laughed, "I know we look alike but you have to be able to tell the difference since you're her man."

Najid frowned, "This is crazy. I didn't know Saadri had a sister. What are you doing out here?"

"I live up the street. I know, we live so close, it's a long story. Pe'r was a busy man." Teran pointed up the block toward her building.

"My mother is Nadine Scott Gregory. Mon mon Ellie is Saadri's mother. We also go to the same school, Prep, but Saadri is a year ahead of me."

"This is crazy, you two could be twins and you are telling me you're from two different mothers?" Najid cocked his head.

Teran laughed and adjusted her shoulder bag. "We get that all of the time. Listen, I have to go because I know my mother will be looking for me to come through the door and I don't want her going nut on me so … It was nice meeting you Najid."

Najid shook his head as Teran laughed and walked away. He turned toward the train station yet stole a few backward glances. The token booth clerk was a familiar face who allowed him to sit in the waiting area. Najid opened his paper and snack, prepared to wait.

Franklin Ave. station was unusually crowded. Saadri knew it could only mean the trains were running erratically. She had to allow two trains to leave the station, loaded with people, before she could board. She used the twenty-minute trip to think over the night's events. It hurt to think Najid was valid in his reasoning on the subject of church members, she wanted desperately to prove church was worthwhile. Saadri sighed as she thought of how hard it was to get a wary person to believe that all church folks weren't hypocritical and snooty when even she was regularly confronted with examples of it. At that point, Saadri determined it was time for Najid and Mary Clark to meet one another. Miss Mary was wise, objective and straightforward, if anyone could convince Najid, it would be Miss Mary.

The train pulled into Rockaway Ave. station at eight thirty in the evening. Saadri left the platform with a light heart for the first time since the incident at the church. As she came through the door into the waiting area she smiled brightly.

Najid folded his paper and stood, wearing a lopsided grin he mouthed, "Candy."

Saadri walked toward him. "What are you doing here?"

"I just felt like you'd be home soon so I waited here for you," Najid kissed her lips briefly.

Saadri was astonished, "How'd you know I'd be home at this time?"

Najid laughed, "I took a chance and waited. I had my munchies and paper to keep me company. Like I said, I just had this feeling you would come at this time. I do remember you telling me you go down to your church on Monday nights."

Saadri kissed him again, "You're amazing; you know that don't you?"

Najid snorted, "I try to be. Listen; do you have a little time to come with me to Eric and Chianna's crib? I wanted to check out the babies and give Eric something to help out with expenses. I haven't seen them yet and I don't know when I'll have an early night again."

Saadri was elated, "Ooh, yes! I haven't seen them either. Wait! I don't have anything to give them!"

Najid soothed, "I have it covered baby."

Saadri objected, "You don't have to -"

Najid looked her in the eye, "I thought we went over this Candy? I'm your man and I will do for you, right?"

The question caused Saadri to come to terms with her need for independence. She knew the tendency had to be curbed in order to solidify their relationship. "You're right baby. Thank you."

"Don't thank me; it's what I'm supposed to do." He guided them through the gate. "Guess who I ran into on my way over here."

Saadri's eyes widened as she formed an 'O' with her mouth. "Who?"

He admired her lips and took the liberty of kissing them before responding, "Teran. I thought she was you and that you were ignoring me. She was walking up Dumont."

"You met Sè?! I know you must have thought you were losing your mind or someone was trying to run game on you." Saadri chuckled, "She is my younger sister, the baby actually - of my father's three girls."

Najid shook his head, "Your pops had three girls?! Any boys?"

"Non, people say we are his chickens come home to roost." Saadri wrapped an arm around Najid's waist as they walked.

He was surprised by the display of affection but he enjoyed it so in turn wrapped an arm around her shoulder. "You got my reaction right. I thought you were playing games but when she kept talking I started figuring out the differences. Why haven't I met her before?"

Saadri wrinkled her nose, "The opportunity just hasn't presented itself. Terry and I are actually very close. Our family calls us twins or Doublemint – Terry can't stand that name though." She laughed at the memory. "I will have to show you the photo albums so you can see us as we grew up. There's a picture of us at about two and three hugging one another and we really looked alike there. We got our Doublemint title because our older sister Veronique couldn't say devilment."

Najid laughed, "So you two were Dennis the Menace in female forms?"

"Non, we weren't the Raenier boys by a long shot. Granmè and Pe'r wouldn't have stood for that." She winked when she finished the statement and playfully pinched his waist.

"You are full of surprises tonight Candy, what's gotten into you?" He kissed her again.

Saadri relayed her evening as they walked toward the Van Dyke housing building where Eric and Chianna resided. Najid stopped her several times trying to fathom the events that unfolded at the church.

"He did what? Look, we can go back up there right now and straighten him out. His daddy obviously doesn't know what's up with his son!"

"Najid stop! This is ridiculous! I told you the pastor pulled him into the office as I left. He will take care of his own son."

Najid spat, "Yeah, but, I'm tired of those people thinking they're better than I am because they sit up in that church. They're going home to the projects just like I am and probably will be for longer than I will. And their kids are out here doing the same thing everyone else is doing and hiding behind God's grace to cover for their misdeeds."

Saadri instantly regretted telling Najid about the incident although it was not her practice to be dishonest with him. His reaction pushed him further away from the church when she wanted the opposite to happen. "Najid, the church is about serving God Almighty. You can't let narrow-minded people get in the way of that. If I allowed everyone's actions and words to sway me, we wouldn't be together."

Najid looked pensively, "What drew you to me Saadri? Why are you with me?"

Saadri saw pain cross Najid's usually stoic features and it rent her heart. That night she made inroads with regard to Najid's character and well-hidden sensitivity. "I'm with you because I know you are a highly capable man who wants more out of life than our present circumstances. You are not afraid to work hard for what you want and you are able to look introspectively to make adjustments when you need to. You are a strong man Najid and that's admirable in this day and time. Most of all, I love you and no one is going to make me stop."

Najid's eyes sparkled, "You make your man feel ten feet tall girl. You're definitely a keeper."

Saadri responded, "Forever."

He guided them into the building and to the elevator. He was relieved no one decided to use the elevator for a bathroom, as was so often the case in their building. He held Saadri close as he pressed the eleventh floor button. When the door slid closed and the two were ensconced within each other's warmth, Najid looked into Saadri's upturned face.

Her eyes held questions and Najid was certain they'd find the answers - together. He watched her a few moments and saw a young woman who'd taken some hard blows from life but still managed to remain standing. She often spoke of her faith in God and Najid admired that she exhibited it in every aspect of her life. Saadri helped him to remember to hold onto his own belief in God. Looking into her hazel eyes Najid loved and respected her on a deeper level. He lowered his head and sighed when she accepted his searching kiss. The elevator reached the eleventh floor much too soon.

Saadri walked out ahead of Najid. He placed both hands on her shoulders to steer her in the direction of the apartment. Before they came to the door he turned her around to face him and kissed her again. "I want you to know I really love you Candy. I respect you for the woman you've turned into and I love you for being with me. If there's anything you want or need, don't ever hold out on me. Understand?" Saadri nodded, too choked up to speak. Najid realized the gravity of the moment and embraced her. They knocked on the door after she was able to compose herself.

Eric's appearance surprised Saadri. He grew a beard and his eyes looked as if they could stand to be closed for a little while. Yet he greeted them with a warm smile.

"What's up? Come in. Long time no see Ace! How are you doing Saadri? You're looking as good as ever. Chianna will be happy to see you; we were just talking to Angelina the other day about you. She said she hadn't been able to catch up to you. Come in folks; make yourself at home. I'll get Chi and the babies."

Eric walked to the back of the two-bedroom apartment while Najid and Saadri settled on an old but comfortable couch. Eric's parents left most of their furniture behind. The whirl of a siren in the street below brought Najid's attention to the circumstances in which Eric and Chianna were raising two baby boys. The reality disturbed him. He looked at Saadri who was studying photographs on the wall before them and knew he didn't want that for them.

Eric and Chianna appeared around the wall, each carrying a son. Saadri stood and squealed with delight, "Ooh, the babies, ahh precious ones. Let me wash my hands, you know I have to hold them!"

Chianna laughed, "Okay girl, down the hall to your left."

Saadri raced off as Najid looked on in amazement. He turned to Eric and questioned, "What is it about babies that makes women change their voice and their whole demeanor?"

Eric laughed, "Man, I can't call it!" He held his son toward Najid, "Ace, this is Jakeem, he was born first."

Saadri bounded into the living room as Najid reached for the baby, "Not before you wash your hands Mister! That baby is too new to be getting your nasty germs! Give me that baby!" She took command of the two men quickly, "Eric, help Chianna sit down, she's having trouble. Najid, the bathroom is down the hall." He watched her for a moment before obediently attending to his sanitary duties.

Eric helped Chianna into a seat before leaving the ladies. She began to address Saadri, "That's Jakeem you have. This one is Jaquan. I can't believe I actually have two sons."

Saadri smiled, "Girl you definitely have a double portion! They are beautiful Chianna. How are you and Eric making out? He looked a little tired when we came through the door. Do you two need me to come sit one night on the weekend so you can get some rest? I really don't mind."

Najid walked into the living room behind Eric, who also heard Saadri, felt his heart burst with pride over her generosity. He added. "We can be here in no time and let you guys get some sleep. I do mean sleep! We won't be watching these two so you guys can go and make number three!" Everyone laughed.

Eric answered, "That's cool of you and your girl Ace, and we'll have to let you know. It's kind of hard to leave them when they're so little. Chianna probably wouldn't let me get any rest asking about them every minute of the hour."

Najid eased onto the couch next to Saadri and watched her as she cradled the sleeping Jakeem in her arms. Her gentleness and agility with the infant moved him. Saadri searched his face and smiled. Their eyes seemed to communicate many pledges of a future together. Najid became excited and wary at once. Instinct and premonition let him know their love would only survive at a steep price, something he couldn't quite figure out yet but he was sure it loomed ahead. He was willing to pay that price but he had to be sure Saadri was ready to pay it also.

One hour later, Saadri and Najid were headed toward their building.

Chapter 9

"Najid, will you come in for a few minutes with me this evening? There's someone I want you to meet."

"It's late, are you sure your mother would appreciate me in her house this time of night?" Najid guided them through the front door of the building.

Saadri stopped him just inside the vestibule, "You're always saying that church people are phony, I just want you to meet one that's up front. So, how about it?"

Najid acquiesced, "Okay, I just hope your moms won't be upset about me being in the house so late."

Mary closed the door to Ellen's bedroom and walked toward the dining room when the front door opened. She walked into the living room and met Saadri. "Where in the world have you been? I thought you would have been in here a while ago." She then looked at the young man standing protectively behind Saadri. "Who's that with you? Turn on the light."

Saadri turned on a nearby lamp and spoke merrily, "Miss Mary, I wanted you to meet Najid-" Saadri looked from Mary to Najid and could sense the tension in the room. Neither of them would disengage their eyes. A sinking feeling settled over her. With far less exuberance, she continued, "Najid this is Mother Mary Clark, she is a member of my church and also my mother's nurse."

Mary spoke, "It's kind of late for Saadri to be getting in the house on a school night."

Najid stared at the older woman, he thought her to be meddlesome and opinionated – just like the older women in their building. Nevertheless, he would not disrespect her, he was taught better. Najid set his mind to showing Mary Clark that he was someone who could not be scared away because of a few well-placed Bible verses. He would not allow her or anyone else make him feel less than the hardworking, driven man he was. Najid tilted his head upward.

Mary placed a hand on her hip as she watched him look at her in defiance. A street thug, that's what he was, and he had the nerve to have naïve Saadri's nose wide open. The young man stepped into Ellen's house like he owned it and she didn't like it one bit. Mary raised her head as well. "Where do you live Najid?"

"I stay with my parents on the fifth floor."

Mary's eyes narrowed, "How old are you?"

Najid maintained eye contact, "I will be twenty-two on February 16th. Once I finish school I will move out of my parents' home."

"You're still in high school?" Mary wore an incredulous expression.

Najid snorted in derision, "No, I attend Baruch College and I have a full-time job so it's taking me longer to graduate. When I do graduate, I'll have a degree in finance and business management."

Mary sat on the couch, "Have a seat son." Najid placed himself comfortably in a seat and guided Saadri to sit next to him; he held her hand as he stared at Mary.

Mary watched him handle Saadri like a puppet and it disturbed her. Najid gazed at Saadri and Mary knew he was communicating with those looks. Whatever they meant, Saadri followed as if in a trance. The power he wielded over the young woman she considered a granddaughter unnerved Mary. The best way to separate the two was to expose Najid for the trouble that he was. "What do you intend to do when you come out of school?"

Najid answered snidely, "Get as far away from here as possible."

Saadri heard Miss Mary gasp but made no move to intervene. Somehow the events that transpired had nothing to do with her. The two squared off and Saadri could only guess they somehow had an earlier meeting. She almost couldn't contain her disappointment. The very things she grew up believing in began to unravel before her. Mary's harsh words broke through her reverie. "What's so wrong with here? Here is where you've grown up, isn't it?"

Najid sat forward and spoke clearly, "There are too many crabs in a barrel, too many hypocrites and too many doom speakers. No one wants to see anyone else get even the smallest amount of good fortune. Everyone wants to hide behind something as an excuse not to get up and try to do something to better the conditions they live within. People always wait on something or someone to come rescue them when it's all up to what they are willing to work for."

Mary sat up, "You speak like you think you are better than everyone else."

Najid shook his head as he sat back on the couch. "No, I'm just willing to work hard."

Mary pointed a finger. "You can't do a thing without God giving you strength in your body. Everyone doesn't have that."

Najid nodded again, "I recognize my life and abilities as gifts from the Almighty. My focus now is to try and do the right things with what He gave me. Everyone doesn't have the strength, but most do and they choose to do nothing with it. I can't sit around and blame my laziness on someone else."

Mary focused in on one of his comments. "What do you mean by now you're trying to do right?"

Najid never flinched, "That means I have had to make some adjustments in my lifestyle and they have been made. I look forward to a positive future and with this pretty lady by my side I know we'll go far."

Mary craned her neck, "The past has a way of catching up with you. You reap what you sow."

Najid nodded, "That's very true, I can attest to that first hand."

"How so?" Mary was determined to expose Najid's misdeeds.

"I have had a few incidences but that's over with now. It's common in these times." Najid shrugged as he made his last statement.

Mary leaned forward, "So you just accept trouble you have gotten into? You don't think it was your fault?"

Saadri stood, "I think that is enough for one night. This is too much for me. First at the church and now you two." She realized she said too much as both Mary and Najid were standing, staring at her with concern.

Najid was about to speak when Mary cut in, "What is the matter sugar? What happened to you tonight?"

Najid answered, "She was accused at church by her pastor because of her pastor's son. Some things you can't control for, even in the church. One well-placed or purposely misplaced word and you stand accused. It's no different than out here in the street."

Mary raised her voice, "Don't you try to compare the church with the street! They are not the same, your deeds have gotten you in trouble and now you are trying to influence this child. Well she has too much going for her to be-"

Saadri felt her patience give out. "Look, I am tired. I just want to take a hot shower and get in bed. Najid, I'll talk to you tomorrow. Miss Mary, I'll call your cab as soon as I let Najid out." She turned and walked toward the door.

Najid stood and looked at Saadri; he could see the fatigue in her frame. Before he walked toward the door he turned to Mary, "How do you know Saadri hasn't been a good influence on me? It was interesting talking to you. Get home safe."

Saadri held her head down; she could feel Najid's anger as he approached. He seethed; Saadri knew it without looking. At the door he passed through and turned toward her once on the other side. "Hold your head up, you have no reason to let it hang; stop trying to prove a point to me that can't be proven right now."

Saadri answered, "Najid, I just don't want you going around not liking God-."

Najid interrupted, "I never told you I didn't like God. My problem is with the people in the church who make a joke out of who God is. We will talk later, count on it." He kissed Saadri's forehead and ascended the stairs toward the fifth floor.

Mary's voice reached Saadri as she closed the door. "I am going outside to wait for the cab. They said one was already in the area and should be around in three to five minutes."

Saadri grabbed her coat and keys and walked out to the vestibule to watch for a cab with Mary. Within three minutes, they saw a Black Pearl logo. Mary opened the vestibule door; a gust of New York wind – the hawk reminded them winter was not yet ready to leave.

Mary turned toward Saadri, "Daughter, you know I want the best for you, don't you?" Saadri nodded. Mary then spoke abruptly, "He's not the best" and left the vestibule.

Saadri watched her get into the cab before she retreated to her apartment. The best, Saadri sighed, could be staring Miss Mary and the rest of the Nay Sayers in the face and they wouldn't know it.

----------◊◊◊----------

Late Spring 1983

The spring semester progressed quickly toward graduation but not without incident. Cedric Sailor died of a drug overdose and Saadri sickened of the great pains church members took to hide the fact. Pastor Sailor himself spoke little if anything about the incident or Cedric. Mary and Najid openly demonstrated their disdain for one another while Saadri did what she could to keep them separated. Mon mon Ellen was hospitalized because of an infection and the doctors predicted her death to occur before the summer ended; however, God was merciful. When she recovered, her organs were strong and the cancer went into remission. Mary's services were no longer needed and the tension in the house dissipated with her departure.

At the same time, her youngest sister, Teran, had gone wild with partying, drinking, and talking to assorted guys after a bad break up with Bashan. Saadri tried to talk with Teran about giving her life to Jesus but her younger sister would not hear her. She finally enlisted the help of Teran's best friend Fawn to encourage her to stop drinking and slow down. Fawn's words and Saadri's threat to call their father ended Teran's hedonism.

Eric Sailor, on the other hand, was a breath of fresh air. One evening, they went to dinner to celebrate his early entrance into Morehouse. He spoke candidly, "You know Saadri; I've watched you ever since your mother became really ill. You developed into a woman of a caliber that is unlike anything to hit that church. That's why everyone has so much to say; they don't know how to deal with you. You know a few of the Elders and Mothers tried to tell me I should stay with my dad because of what happened with Cedric? The truth is, Cedric was always the most selfish and overindulged of my brothers and sisters. He always had to get the attention and he tried to do next to nothing for anyone else. Don't get me wrong, I loved my brother but he was weak and he was permitted to stay weak while the rest of us had to measure up to standards." Saadri watched Eric, trying to digest his words.

Eric recognized her struggle and clarified, "What I'm trying to say to you Saadri is that you know things are shaky out here. I hope to God that when I get to Georgia I can find something better. Dad and Mom will make it and the same people will be at the church doing the same thing. You and I serve a great big God and there's no reason why we can't go and see what's out there. Who knows, we might mess around and get blessed!" Saadri laughed as Eric continued, "Your boyfriend how is he?"

Saadri gave Eric a warm smile, "Najid is just fine. I don't get to see him as much as I'd like. Between school and his job, he gets home pretty late."

Eric teased, "I see he still has you grinning like you hit the number. That's good; he's had a positive effect on you. Listen, Cedric knew your boyfriend. The night we ran into him at the train station, Cedric told me after you two left. I'm sure you know that dude used to be into some heavy stuff back in the day. How Cedric knew, I'm sure you're wondering. He was in it himself. They had some rival run-ins and even got busted in the same group once. Cedric also told me dude had gone straight, little did I know my brother hadn't."

Eric paused to be sure his words sank in. "Saadri someone helped my brother take his last breath. The autopsy stated that strychnine was present in his blood stream. My dad didn't want to follow up on it because he said losing his son was painful enough. I don't even think anyone at the church knows that fact. There's a lot that goes on no one either talks about or knows about."

Saadri sighed, "I guess you really needed to purge. Here I was thinking you'd want to celebrate your last few weeks in town. That was insensitive of me, I'm sorry."

Eric waved his hands, "No, that's not it at all. I'm just using this opportunity to tell you I want you to get out of here, get out of East New York. Go somewhere other than New York and take Najid with you. This is not living, it's existing. Get out and find some happiness."

Saadri was thankful to have a friend like Eric and she told him so before they settled down to a hearty meal.

Graduation arrived with a flurry of activity. Her father and grandmother flew in from Louisiana and stayed at the apartment. More than the previous time he'd come, Damas made overtures toward Ellen. They spent a lot of time together and went on two dates besides the family dinner where he also had Teran and Najid along. Mazie took one look at Najid and kissed his cheek calling him one of her fiy or children. Damas and Najid hit it off and Saadri was relieved to have her father's approval. Ellen seemed to relax more with Damas' approval as well. Saadri prayed that with her improved health she would have clarity of mind to take a chance with her lifelong love.

Saadri stood in her room checking her attire in the floor length mirror Najid purchased as a gift. Najid arrived over a half-hour earlier and sat in the living room talking with Damas and Ellen. Mazie helped Teran with her toilette as she had when they were all little girls and as she had when they were readying for special occasions. It was a Villere and Buard tradition. Saadri heard them laugh about something and smiled to herself. She opened her bedroom door and stepped out into the hall.

Najid whistled when Saadri entered the room in a coral silk dress. The dress was her graduation gift from his mother Margie. "Girl, you look so good, you belong on a runway modeling."

Saadri laughed. "I am far from modeling material but thanks for the compliment anyway."

Damas rebutted, "Of course you are Shaer! Mo fiy çé bèl!" (My daughter is beautiful!)

Najid did not quite understand the language but grasped the proud father's context before adding, "Yes, my Creole baby is fine." He nodded toward Damas who tipped his head in Najid's direction.

Ellen held out a manicured hand for her daughter, "Well this is it; you're stepping with the big dogs now. I am proud of you Saadri and I love you dearly. Where's the camera, I want to take a picture of you."

Chapter 10

Najid grabbed his camera from the kitchen table just as the front door opened to everyone's surprise. He and Mary looked at one another with contempt. Damas saw the exchange. "Why did you use the key?" Ellen frowned but remained silent; she never could stand up to Damas. Mazie looked on from her seat at the kitchen table.

Mary blustered, "Well I had a key because I was taking care of Evangelist Weston. I wanted to see Saadri off today."

"You didn't answer my question." Damas' look bore holes through Mary's defense.

"I apologize, I had the key and was used to using it so I just came on in to see the baby off and check on Sis Ellie."

Ellen spoke jovially, "Well, you're in the house now so let's take some pictures. This is my baby's day and I want it to be special."

Mary removed a manila envelope from her large bag and extended it to Saadri with a slight tremor in her hand. "I won't be staying; I just wanted to make sure Saadri had these blessings from Pastor, me, and some of the other members." She kissed Saadri's cheek and hugged her. "You mind if I pray for her?"

Ellen held Damas' hand as she answered, "We would like that Mother Clark, thank you."

Mary took both of Saadri's hands and commenced. "Heavenly Father, we come to You in praise and thanksgiving for such a momentous day. We ask you to look over Saadri and make this a blessed and wonderful occasion for her. Father we pray You shield her from the wolves that come to devour. We ask that You would keep her alert and discerning as she goes through not only this day but all the days to come, be with her in the dark times and bring her through every test triumphantly. Remove every stain and dark root trying to choke life from her but cause her to rise up in victory and refreshing, we pray. Thank you for her life, health, and strength. In Jesus name, amen."

The room remained silent once Mary finished and Ellen kept her eyes closed. "Thank you Mother Clark."

Damas turned toward Ellen but her eyes were still closed so he didn't speak. Mary looked at Saadri a final time and whispered, "We are here for you baby so never hesitate to call on us." The woman turned toward the door as she reached in her bag and walked up to Damas, "Here is the house key, congratulations to everyone on the big day. God bless you all."

"Mother Clark, thank you for everything you have done and been for us." Ellen took the older woman by the hands.

"Evangelist Weston it was my pleasure and I thank God for your healing. We all do and we are looking forward to more ministry with you." They hugged and Ellen walked her to the door.

Damas slipped the key in his pocket and turned to Saadri. "Fiy, we need to get going."

Ellen came back with, "Hey, hey! I still have to take pictures." She called her preferences as the family posed: Saadri with her parents; Saadri with each parent; Saadri with her grandmother; Najid and Damas; Najid, Damas, and Mazie; Najid, Damas, Mazie, and Saadri; Najid, Ellen, Mazie, and Saadri; and finally – Najid and Saadri.

Ellen watched as Najid moved behind Saadri. He protectively wrapped his arms around her waist and rested his chin on her right shoulder. Tears pooled as she remembered... It was evident the young man loved her daughter. Saadri's animation as she adoringly watched his every move let Ellen know her daughter also loved Najid. Ellen prayed that long after she was gone from the earth their love would remain. "Say cheese."

Damas took the camera and kissed Ellen's tears. He tried not to show relief when she did not resist, he took her mouth. No one in the room stirred. Najid held onto Saadri before she moved to her parents, "Now let me take a picture of you and Pe'r, Mon mon."

Ellen started to protest but Saadri smiled, "Come on now, it's my graduation day." They smiled and she took the picture.

Damas announced, "Okay, let's round it up. I am going to get the car and bring it to the front so be outside in about five minutes." Najid left with him.

The women stepped into a crisp and comfortable morning. Rasheen and his parents, Jack and Margie, stood in the courtyard talking; they turned and smiled. "Congratulations!" rang out from the Raeniers as they walked toward Saadri. The group hugged and Saadri watched Najid walk up the path toward her.

"It's time to step into the next phase of life Candy. Are you ready?" He stopped a little away from the group and stood with his arm extended toward her. Rasheen stood by watching.

Saadri looked at Najid in a rust t-shirt under a cream linen suit with matching rust loafers and black sunglasses waiting for her to come to him. His flat top was naturally curly and the sun exposed his hair's jet black color and sheen to perfection. She swallowed. The question meant more than Najid dared say in front of others. She stepped forward and took his hand. Rasheen smiled.

He led them away from the building. Calls of congratulations proceeded from people in their windows. Saadri saw a white stretch limousine and looked at Najid.

He smiled, "I told you I would give you the world girl. Today you're riding in style." Margie Raenier and Ellen took a picture of the car and the couple with the car before they left.

Damas hustled Ellen and his mother into the car he rented and made ready for downtown Brooklyn. He was about to pull off when he spotted running figures.

Inside the limo Najid pulled Saadri close to his side. "A penny for your thoughts..."

Saadri turned toward him, "I love you. No one has ever done the things for me that you do."

Najid held her hands, "There's more coming Candy. This is only the beginning."
He kissed her briefly and settled them into the limo.

Saadri looked out of her window and jumped out of the car. "Sè! Aou to va?"

Najid stepped out of the car and saw Teran and another beauty standing on the sidewalk out of breath. Saadri bounded toward them and screamed, "Veronique!"

Damas yelled, "Get in this car! We will be late! Why can't I get you to be anywhere on time? I was about to leave the both of you."

The young women spoke in unison, "Wi Pe'r." and walked to the car briskly.

Najid resettled Saadri into the limo. "Is the blonde the other sister you told me about?"

"That's Veronique, she is the oldest by six months and she will be here for the summer so you'll get plenty of time to know her." Saadri snuggled into his outstretched arm.

After the graduation ceremony, Najid surprised Saadri with a gold bracelet. Damas looked at the piece of jewelry appreciatively if not a bit skeptically. He was also reluctant to let Saadri leave but Ellen reminded him that she was out of school and eighteen which gave her latitude to make her own decisions. He drove his family back to Brownsville with a sour expression on his face.

Saadri and Najid went into Manhattan and had a celebratory lunch near Fiftieth Street on the west side of town. Afterward they strolled and window shopped as Najid questioned, "Where do you see us in the future?"

Saadri raised her eyebrows, "I would want to be married."

Najid nodded his head in agreement, "Me too. When?"

Saadri's brows knit together, "When what?"

"When do we get married?" Najid stood in front of her, expecting an answer.

With a smile Saadri challenged, "Today. Now."

Najid steered them to a phone booth and made a call. Saadri's heart pumped wildly. He came out of the booth and stated, "We need get you a ring before we catch a bus up to Connecticut. I have a friend up there who will be a witness for us. There's no waiting period. We need to stop and get some clothes to change into also."

Saadri walked with her hand inside Najid's large one as if she were dazed. They entered a jewelry store and sized Saadri's ring finger. When they agreed upon a trio of yellow gold bands Najid whipped out a gold credit card.

"Working on Wall Street has really paid off for you, hasn't it?" Saadri questioned as they exited the store.

Najid squeezed the hand he held gently, "Those are the first words you've uttered since we agreed to get married. Are you still willing to go through with this?" He watched Saadri's face intently.

She knew she had to answer carefully, "This has come as a complete surprise. I graduated from high school less than four hours ago and now I'm about to get married. I don't even know where we'll live or anything."

Najid thought about her words, "Maybe I am rushing you. I just want you to know I am serious about us. Why don't we wait until you are really sure about the right time to do this? Meanwhile, we can become engaged. How does that sound?"

"I think that sounds wonderful. I love you Najid. I just want to make sure I am a good and ready wife for you... So, the bus ride should be enough time to get used to the idea." Saadri kissed his lips. Najid grinned as he watched Saadri pull away from the brief kiss. "Let's get going before you have second thoughts. This has to be the most spontaneous I have ever been."

Najid looked at Saadri to make sure she understood her decision. "You still have time to change your mind."

Saadri smiled, "Najid, I have never been surer of anything in my life. I am not about to change my mind. The question is, are you getting cold feet?"

Najid laughed and held her hand to his heart. "I'm making you a promise baby. We will have a beautiful life together. In the meantime Miss Buard, I need to ask if you would marry me and share the rest of our lives together."

Saadri grinned, "Yes Mr. Raenier, I will marry you."

"Then I believe this ring is yours." Najid slipped the gold one-carat ring onto Saadri's sized five finger. He then looked into her eyes, "Now you have proof of my love for you. No matter what anyone might say, I am for real about us."

"For the record, I didn't need this ring as a reminder of our feelings for one another. They are with me even when you're not. As for what others might say, I told you before that I don't pay them any mind."

Najid placed a large neatly manicured hand on Saadri's cheek. "You are one extraordinary woman Saadri Isaure Buard, soon-to-be Raenier. With you I can believe in so much. I love you with all I know how girl. Don't ever forget it."

"I love you right back Najid Amaury Raenier. Don't you ever forget that!"

They went to Grand Central Station and caught the Conrail to Connecticut where Mr. Grey met them. He witnessed the two become Mr. and Mrs. Raenier by six that evening. The older man gifted them with a hotel stay and dinner.

Summer 1983

Najid seemed to walk on cloud nine as he received the support of family and friends. While Ellen gleamed over the news, she openly admitted to being unhappy with Saadri's decision not to tell Damas, Mazie, or her sisters. Ellen was further unhappy about Saadri not telling the members of the church. Joining Ellen in her disenchantment was Najid who couldn't understand why Saadri wanted their marriage to remain a secret. He was bothered but decided to give his wife the time she needed to open up about their relationship. Saadri settled with the fact that when Damas found out there would be fireworks so she decided to prolong the day of reckoning, focus on her marriage, and enjoy her older sister visiting with her for the summer.

Veronique called out, "I'll get it Mon mon Ellie!" Through the peephole she watched Najid remove his Kangol and wipe his face with a handkerchief. She opened the door with a smile, "Hey Hardrock! You look hot. Come on in, although, it's not that much better. We have a million fans blowing hot air around."

"Goldilocks!" He kissed the attractive young woman's cheek. "Where's my wife?"

Veronique looked at him with a frown, "You're wife? You two are just in love to the max, aren't you? She was in the shower but she is probably out by now or do you want to jump in with her?" Najid wiggled an eyebrow and they shared a laugh. "I bet you do but Mon mon Ellie is not going for any premarital horizontal in her house so you better chill out boy."

"Stop being so jealous Nique. If you would behave yourself one of my homeboys would rap to you. You're too uptight." He pinched one of her arms.

"You don't have a homeboy I want a rap from, really! And I'm not uptight, it's called having standards and I don't understand why my sister relaxed hers." She walked away from the door and left Najid to lock it.

He laughed as he watched her, "See, that's what I'm talking about, too much mouth and too many insults. How is a man supposed to be attracted to all of that mouth Nique? I know what's wrong though, you haven't done the nasty yet. I know you Buard girls are good girls cause Papa Damas got y'all crapping bricks!" He laughed aloud.

Veronique whirled on a hip and replied, "Don't worry about my private affairs and you'd better not be bothering my little sister about all of that business either!"

Najid frowned. "Take a chill pill Nique. You girls are too high strung. Where's the Twin? I'm surprised she is not up in here with y'all. I usually find the trio all together when I come up in here."

"She was running around with her girlfriend Fawn last night so she's in Crown Heights. She'll surface sooner or later; she's the gypsy like her mother."

Saadri walked out of the bathroom and into the bedroom wrapped in a towel. She looked over her shoulder, "Hey baby! I missed you today. I'll be right out."

Najid inwardly groaned, "Don't take too long. I missed you too."

"Oh gag me with a spoon! Y'all are too much." Veronique left the living room area to enter the kitchen as Najid threw a couch pillow that landed in the middle of her back.

"No you didn't just throw this at me!" She missiled the pillow before she finished her response and Najid caught it, with a lopsided grin. She sucked her teeth and walked into the kitchen.

"Why are you teasing that child? You like to have her upset and carrying on Najid." Ellen shook her head as she walked toward her son-in-law.

As they hugged Najid whispered, "Ma Ellie she still doesn't know we're married?" Ellen shook her head and Najid frowned.

She whispered in return, "You and Saadri have to talk about this because it can't be a secret from everyone too much longer."

"What are you two conspiring about?" Saadri smiled as she watched her mother and husband. When she saw Najid's face the smile faltered.

Ellen touched her arm, "You two need to talk. Nique! What are you doing in there? Come on and let's go up to Manhattan, I feel like dinner and a movie."

Veronique appeared with a sandwich in hand. "That sounds good! Do you want me to call and see if Teran is back?"
Ellen nodded as she walked toward her bedroom, "Yeah that would be nice, the three of us can hang out."

"Okay." Veronique looked from Saadri to Najid, "Remember what I said Hard Rock."

He smirked.

Chapter 11

Najid sat on the side of the full sized bed in Saadri's room, their room, and stretched.

"I guess you really did miss me." Saadri giggled as she lay on a pillow, her mussed hair fell haphazardly.

"You have no idea how sexy you are Mrs. Raenier." He playfully pulled at the sheet.

She smiled, "I am only concerned that you keep that sentiment Mr. Raenier."

He leaned over and grabbed her mouth in a kiss that left her winded. "You have no need to worry that I won't. Are you hungry? I know I am. I have to keep my strength up, messing with you." She traced a finger along his jawline, through his neatly trimmed facial hair. Saadri knew he found it stimulating and she grinned when Najid closed his eyes. "Candy, you know what you're doing." He stopped her hand. "I want to go get something to eat and talk to you."

"I guess I can no longer keep you distracted." She gently pulled her hand away and sat up. "Can we go to Steve's on Third Avenue or the Blue Bird Diner in Flatlands?"

Najid opened his eyes and stared into her green pupils – still excited from their intimacy. "I think Blue Bird will be better since it's closer. We'll be starving after we're done."

Chris Hanley nearly stumbled when he saw Veronique Buard walk out of a corner store near Dumont Ave. He made his way across the street. "Hello!"

Saadri Raenier looked into his face and the recognition was evident, "Hello?"

The young man straightened, "You're Ace's girl, right?"

Saadri stifled the urge to correct him, "Yes." She stared at Chris.

He looked into her hazel eyes and shifted from her to Veronique. "I see why he has you. I saw your friend here –"

"My sister."

Veronique watched the exchange as Teran bounded from the store, "Okay, let's hit it!"

Chris gasped, "She has to be your sister too cause you two look just alike!" He looked at Saadri who nodded. "Sisters! Y'all have to be the finest chicks out here in the Ville!"

"We're no one's chicks, we're women. We are also leaving." Teran motioned her sisters toward the train station.

"Nice to meet y'all. Have fun and don't worry, no one will mess with any of you out here. I have y'all back." Chris folded his arms and nodded.

Saadri answered, "That won't be necessary but thank you."

He shook and responded, "You tell Ace I said I am looking out for y'all."

His stance let Saadri know there was more behind the young man's declaration. She responded "Thank you."

"You're Saadri but what are your sister's names?" He nodded in their direction.

Saadri pointed, "This is Veronique and this is Teran."

"It's nice to meet you Veronica and Terry. Are y'all French or something?"

"I am Veronique and we are Creole." She lifted her head.

"Although they call me Terry, I am Teran."

Chris snapped his fingers, "I know you! Russell Parks, right?"

Teran lowered her eyes, "Unfortunately."

The young man titled his head, "What's up? He wasn't good to you?"

"It's the past so no need in dredging up old dirt." Teran shifted to a hip.

"Miss Veronique, I've never talked to a Creole girl before." He stared directly at the one who'd gotten his initial attention.

Veronique watched his demeanor and knew he was not a bum but she knew he was not a keeper either. "Well, this is your lucky day because you're talking to three of them."

He smiled again, "You're right but it's you I would like to get to know better. Can I take you to a movie, treat you to dinner, or take you out to Coney Island maybe? Whatever you'd like to do, that's what we'll do, okay?"

"Are you sure that won't take you away from watching over the Ville? It's tough to get away with so much responsibility." Veronique smirked.

"Every king needs a queen so how do I get a queen if I don't get away to know one? That being said, I will gladly leave my post to spend some time with you. Do I get a yes pretty lady?" Chris stepped closer to Veronique.

Saadri bristled, "Nique does not live here so there is no need for this." She stepped behind Chris' line of vision and motioned for her sister to say no. Teran watched with amusement.

Veronique rolled her eyes, "I believe we can arrange something."

Saadri's eyes turned green but she stood and watched the two make plans for a date. After they conferred, Chris turned to her, "Don't worry, I'll be the perfect gentleman with your sister. Y'all have fun tonight and remember I have eyes on you, y'all are safe out here." He turned to Veronique, "I am looking forward to this." He crossed Rockaway Avenue and headed toward Tilden Houses. Saadri swallowed.

"You're not going Nique!" Najid leaned against the living room wall glaring.

Veronique stood from her perch on the arm of the couch. "You may be the king gangster around here but I am not in your gang!"

"You're not going." Najid remained in place.

"I am not your woman!"

"You're not going."

"You don't tell me what to do!"

"You're not going."

Veronique stepped up to Najid, "Just try to stop me." He stood and never broke eye contact, she stepped back. Najid left the apartment without a word.

Teran questioned, "Where is he going? Nique, why do you have to be the b- all the time? He is going out there to confront that dude. Dri already told you they were in rival crews. Could you have not challenged Najid like that for her sake? He has clout out here; you don't understand how things work here in Brooklyn. If there is a war out here you get to go back to North Carolina but we have to stay!"

Veronique hadn't thought about that. She quickly left the house.

Najid motioned for his crew to stop talking as Veronique approached him. The crew watched the tall blonde girl with appreciation but made no overtures except a nod in her direction. She returned their nods and walked up to Najid. They stared at one another a few seconds. "You're out here because?"

With an audible exhale she began, "Okay Najid, you win."

He folded his arms, "You think this is a game?"

"No, I don't." She moved next to him and laid her head on his shoulder. "I just don't like to be controlled."

"Nique, there is a difference between being controlled and being protected. I couldn't live with myself if I allowed something to happen to you." He touched her cheek.

"Can you get me out of it? I don't want a neighborhood brouhaha over me accepting a date with your nemesis."

Najid laughed, "I love the vocabulary that you sisters use. You can sound like college professors sometimes, it's impressive. Don't worry about Chris." Veronique returned to the apartment concerned for her sister.

Saadri, Teran, and Veronique stood in the airport lobby hugging. Ellen announced, "She's not leaving forever, my goodness!" She took pictures of the threesome until it was time for Veronique to board the plane.

"Saadri please be careful okay? Najid is into some heavy stuff and I don't want you to suffer for it. These New York guys are a trip. I will stick with my Southern boys."

Teran interjected, "Nique, not all New York guys are hard rocks or women beaters. We have some really good guys too."

Veronique looked at Teran's barely veiled turmoil and felt her insides melt, "I wish you could come back with me Terry but I have to start school and I won't have the time to spend with you like I would want. Listen, I want you to know things will get better for you. I need you to get your head together because senior year is important. Stop all of that wild partying and drinking girl and carry yourself like a lady or I'm telling Granmè. You know she'll come up here and hustle you down to Louisiana and you'll be graduating from Natchitoches High School!"

Saadri joked, "Then you won't have an excuse not to attend Xavier."

Teran rolled her eyes, "Pe'r called and spoke with me about that just last week. He is seriously trying to make me go there. It's like he won't hear of me going anywhere else. One of you should have gone so I wouldn't be aggravated with this."

Veronique laughed, "Be', welcome to our world. Dri and I always had to make things better for you. This time it's your turn. We don't envy you either because Pe'r is like the Rock of Gibraltar!" They laughed and Nique said her goodbyes.

Mid-August in New York City was especially sticky as the city found itself caught in the middle of a sweltering heat wave. Saadri couldn't get into the building fast enough. The three-block walk from Rockaway Ave. train station to her Blake Ave. apartment building was enough to soak Saadri down to her underwear. All she could think of was a cool shower and the air conditioner Najid purchased for the living room area. The high-powered conditioner was strong enough to cool the entire apartment once turned on.

Saadri made it through the yard without incident. It was, thankfully, too hot for people to be sitting out minding the business of others. She walked into her apartment and found a note on the kitchen table from her mother reminding she would be gone for the next week - she was in Texas with Damas. Saadri grinned as she thought of her parents reconciling. Although Ellen told her not to get her hopes too high, Saadri sensed they would be headed toward the altar soon. She made her way to the shower as she planned how to spend the time with her husband.

Thoughts fought for control of Najid's mind to the point that he didn't notice the town car following him during his evening walking ritual. Mounting stressors in the neighborhood were causing problems with his plan to take Saadri away from Brownsville. He was no fool; it was never easy to walk away from the life he lived. Rival groups and subtle messages being sent from backers were threatening to pull him into the life again. He had too much at stake to allow that to happen. His talk that day with his mentor, Mr. Grey, gave him a ray of hope. Najid felt uneasy for the first time in his life, if he never planned before, this time he needed to.

"Hey Acey-Deucy there!"

Najid inwardly cringed; the town car effortlessly glided to the curb beside him. Najid became fully alert and held onto the hope, desperately, that everything would work out satisfactorily. When the door swung open he began to have his doubts.

The gentleman furthest away from the door Najid entered spoke; there was no mistaking his position of importance. "How are you enjoying your Wall Street job? Do you like it better than the work we had for you these days? Is it making that pretty wife of yours happy?"

Najid spoke without trepidation; any show of weakness would end his life. "Wall Street is good for me. We like it just fine."

The gentleman leaned forward a little, "Well now, as a businessman, what do you propose I do for the threat to revenue your absence has caused?"

Najid knew things weren't going as well with the leadership vacuum his absence created but he reassured the interested parties there was a reasonable amount of turn-around time for profits to again be realized. Maybe he underestimated David Jones' ability to maintain the number one spot. "There are some other options to explore."

The gentleman stated succinctly, "You have one other option to exercise before you go back and take the helm again. Am I clear?"

Najid consented, "Very."

The gentleman smiled, "What is this option?"

Chapter 12

Saadri finished the meal and stood back to view her creation. Her mother would have been proud, especially since she swore Saadri couldn't cook. Keys jangling in the door put an instant smile on her face. She quickly answered, "Hi Baby, I'm glad you could make it!"

Najid grinned, "You just don't know how it makes me feel to see you standing here next to a meal you've prepared."

Saadri walked up and threw her arms around him. "Well, you are my husband and you've worked hard so I want to make sure you get a solid meal."

Najid placed a kiss on her neck, chin and lips, "Yeah, but it feels good for a man to come home to this. I promise you the next few days will be the best we've had yet."

Saadri pressed herself into Najid's chest and they stood embraced for a few moments. She broke with, "I hope you brought an appetite in that door with you. Mon mon doesn't think I can cook but I know how."

Najid rubbed his hands together. "That's because she spoils you and does the cooking herself. Even when she was sick you didn't cook, Broom Hilda did."

"You need to stop; Miss Mary is not here to defend herself." Saadri quickly set silverware on the table and prepared to fix a plate when Najid walked to the bathroom.

"Give me some of everything baby! I see you went all out."

Saadri joked, "Well, I figured I would make enough to last us the weekend. Then I will make a couple of dishes for the week."

Najid sat at the table with his silverware in the air, "If my baby made it, it's good. Let's get it on girl!" He watched the plate expectantly as a smiling Saadri walked it over. "Where's Miss Ellie?"

Saadri set the plate in front of Najid, "You must have forgotten. She's down in Texas with Pe'r."

Najid bellowed, "Hot diggity-dang! Damas that old dawg got her down there. He'll wear down her resistance for sure. I guess we aren't the only ones getting horizontal this weekend!"

"Najid Amaury Raenier! You are talking about my parents!" Saadri stopped with his plate mid-air.

"I'm sorry baby but you are proof that they have been horizontal before." He tried to appear contrite while stifling a grin.

She set the plate down, "No you're not."

He laughed then looked down at his plate of steak, baked potato, and steamed vegetables. "This looks wonderful baby, hurry so we can grace the table."

"Go ahead I don't want you to wait on me. No one likes lukewarm food. Father in Heaven, we thank you for this meal. We thank you for the time we get to spend together and most of all we thank you for your son Jesus. Amen."

The dinner progressed well and Najid cleaned the kitchen while Saadri reclined on the couch where they settled to talk.

"Baby that was a good meal; I am blessed with such a fine woman." Najid stroked Saadri's cheek as he spoke.

"Thank you Baby. You must want something." She chuckled at her humor.

"Yeah dessert." They both laughed before he continued, "Listen Baby, I wanted to really sit down and talk to you about some things. I know your father and sisters don't know about us and I went along because you dealt with me and my issues. Thank you for hanging in there with me. Look, there are some things I have to take care of and I just need your patience."

Saadri frowned, "You alarm me when you're so cryptic. I feel like you're in danger and you don't want me to know."

"Candy, I have been no angel, I'll admit. I've made decisions that I have to cope with but my love and devotion to you has not and will not change. You may not understand or like all I do but know that I protect you."

Saadri's eyes closed, "I get so scared Najid."

"Come here; let me put you at ease."

"Acey-Deucy! How goes it there?!"

Najid turned toward the voice and fought hard to control his shock as he looked across the crowd in Battery Park. There was no way he was going to be pulled into the life again; yet, they were sending clear messages that they controlled his fate. He was glad he already enacted part of his game plan with Mr. Grey. He nodded in the henchman's direction and proceeded to finish his lunch.

The henchman and he never got along and Najid's actions communicated the henchman would have to walk over to him to deliver any messages. The henchman barreled over and sat across from Najid. "Okay smart guy. Look here, the boss is feeling benevolent toward you for some reason I can't seem to figure out. Then again, he always had a soft spot for you."

Najid answered, "It would be unfortunate for him to find out about your feelings regarding his soft spot. What's the message?"

The henchman glared but continued, "There's a price for freedom. You'll have to put in a lot of time to get it." Without another word, the henchman rose and left, but not before Najid could see the grin on his face.

Najid made a show of finishing the lunch he no longer wanted. Mentally, he began to accelerate his plan. There were caveats that needed to be added and they would not be pleasant. He could deal with the displeasures as long as he knew he would still have Saadri.

Chapter 13

Fall 1983

Saadri rode the IRT towards her East New York station, after hanging out one evening with some friends from high school. During the ride, she had time to think about the strain on her and Najid's relationship. His frequent absences left her unsure about their future in spite of the reassurances he gave her that he was working toward their future. As she walked home from her station, Saadri met the subject of her musing.

"Saadri!"

Saadri turned in time to see Najid jump out of a black Mercury. He walked toward her in a gait that did not belie his anger. She stood on the sidewalk nearest their building and waited.

Najid walked into her personal space and Saadri knit her brows. "Where have you been?!" came through clenched teeth.

Saadri was incensed. He offered no kiss and she'd not seen him in four days! "What do you care? You are too busy out here playing the hard rock!" She stepped away from him and began to move toward their building. Najid quickly strode beside her and took her hand. He held it firmly and Saadri knew to withdraw from his touch would mean an ugly confrontation. Najid guided them through the entrance and vestibule then took out his keys to allow them entry to the apartment. Saadri walked in ahead of him and began to disrobe of her outerwear. She took great care hanging her things in the hall closet. When she completed her task she was met with Najid's hand on her arm. She spun toward him quickly.

"I asked you a question. And you know you don't walk away from me. That fool must have filled your head up with much trash tonight."

Saadri could feel her stomach quiver, "What are you talking about?"

"I'm talking about your little boyfriend out in Flatbush tonight!" Najid moved away from her and slapped his hands together.

Saadri watched him in mild shock, "How did you know I was in Flatbush tonight?"

Najid folded his arms across his chest, "There are a lot of things I know that you don't. Now what's up with homeboy? He's giving you attention you feel like you're not getting from me? Is he paying for your clothes and buying food and giving you spending money too?"

Saadri was livid, before she could think better she went into her purse. "You know what? No, he's not paying for anything because he's just an old classmate as well as the rest of them. I guess you want to act like you didn't see the rest of the group I was with. As for all the bills and food and spending money, just tell me what I owe. I like to pay my debts." Saadri held the pen and checkbook open.

Najid nodded his head, "So Papa Damas must have sent you some money and you're ready to grandstand now."

Saadri answered him snidely, "I don't need your money. I have a daddy."

Najid tilted his head to one side, a sure sign he was trying to keep his irritation in check. "You have a husband. That daddy's girl stuff won't wash. Don't try to make me insignificant."

"That's on you, not me. You're the one out hustling and running in the streets doing God knows what else to God knows who else!"

Najid sucked his teeth, "What I do and whom I do it with is none of your business."

"What?!" Saadri could feel a throbbing sensation in her forehead, "When did this come about? Or was this the agenda the whole time?"

"Saadri, I have respected you to the utmost and provided for you. Don't ask me about my business." Najid sat on the couch. "What's in the refrigerator? I'm hungry."

Saadri shifted her weight to one hip and unleashed, "I am not, nor have I ever been one of your street flunkies. I am supposed to be your wife and not too long ago you acted like that meant something to you but I guess your plans have changed. You're too busy being the Godfather again. I am not stupid Najid, you were out there when we first got together but you came out. For some reason known only to God you have found a reason to go back. I can't and I won't sit here and let you drag me into this kind of life. You always knew I wanted more and I thought you did too. I thought we'd do it together. I have given you my love and I have always been supportive of you but I can't do it like this. When are we going to make this marriage real in every sense?"

Najid looked at her. "That's why you never told your father or sisters, right? You never looked at us as real." He nodded and spoke more to himself, "Ain't this a kick in the teeth! You never thought our marriage was real."

He knew what he had to do and he knew the price he'd pay for doing it. It hurt him but he couldn't fold. Saadri deserved better. He stood and approached her. "Saadri, I don't mean to ever hurt you." Her eyes pleaded with him; he knew she was afraid.

As he gathered her in his arms, Saadri felt something indescribable transpire between them. She sensed they both knew it was the beginning of the end. She reached up and kissed him, she couldn't stop even when she registered the intensity change. She would not stop kissing him.

Najid stretched as the sun poured into the bedroom. He looked over at Saadri's sleeping form and his breath caught. He loved her more than he thought he knew how to love. Her outline brought back memories of pleasure and promises, promises he now knew he wouldn't be able to keep. Najid leaned over and kissed her forehead. She stirred and he was desperately misplaced, cursing the law of nature that every choice had a consequence. He placed a hand tenderly on her hip. For one sweet moment, he was making a choice that might be the last thing he did within his control.

Chris Williams stood at the approach of the rival group. His crew positioned themselves, ready to ward off any surprise attack. The meeting was too good to pass up but it could have been a trap. Chris despised Najid; in a perfect world they would have been on the same team, but, two leaders such as they were would never be able to coexist in the same organization. Begrudgingly, Chris respected Najid's commanding presence. Just as he respected the way Najid ran his crew and his family. The way they hustled the sister back to the South and out of his reach checked him; he hated Najid's finesse. If the meeting went well, Chris would become indebted to Najid and that fact added kindling to his banked fire. Such debt would come with unspoken expectations.

Najid insisted they meet in a neutral place. Chris was known for his ruthless nature and Najid wanted to make sure he was on equal footing with his greatest rival. They faced off and Najid took his time speaking, he didn't want the desperate nature of the situation to become apparent to Chris. "Glad you could get here. Like I said, I have an opportunity I think you might find interesting."

Chris nodded slightly, "What will this opportunity cost me?"

Najid responded, "The benefits far outweigh the costs to you. Just 'look out' for some people; that's the only request."

Chris looked at Najid a few moments before he asserted, "If I like what I hear then we have a deal."

In the midst of a game of cat and mouse, Najid attempted to stay a step ahead. The transition went through and seemed to progress smoothly but he remembered there was a price to pay for getting out - putting in some time. He didn't know which way the price would come but he knew it loomed in the future.

Ellen, who started looking pale again, commented, "Look at the sheepskin couple. That coat is about to swallow Saadri, it's so long." She laughed, "Let me get my camera."

They posed for the picture – Najid stood behind and wrapped his arms around his wife. After the snapshot Saadri commented, "We'll be back later tonight Mon mon, don't wait up."

"Enjoy yourselves." Ellen kissed them and escorted them to the door.

They stepped outside the building and the wind whipped across their faces. Najid pulled Saadri closer. I guess Old Man Winter is saying he's coming early and staying long."

Grey Flannel wafted past her nose and Saadri inhaled the masculine scent of her husband. She snuggled closer, "Thanksgiving is still over a week away and it's already 'Who's your Daddy?' weather? Good grief."

Najid laughed, "We'll take a cab home."

He surprised Saadri with tickets to "Amen Corner" on Broadway after his mentor, Phillip Grey, talked about how good the performance was. The look on his wife's face when they arrived and her enjoyment of the musical production let him know he was on the right path in treating her to multiple experiences. They left the theater and went over to the east side, Third Avenue, to Jackson Hole where Najid ordered him and Saadri gourmet cheeseburgers with steak fries and the salad she demanded.

"Candy, I know you are not going to try and eat your burger with a knife and fork? Pick that thing up and bite into it woman!" Najid shook his head as he watched his wife slice her cheeseburger in half.

"This thing is huge; first of all, I would be big as a house eating all of this. Then you would have something to say about the weight I've gained. I'll pick it up but only half of it." She took her time separating the halves and made a show of slowly allowing the burger to approach her mouth. When she took the first bite her eyes closed and she moaned. "This is delicious."

"I have to get you out of here making sounds like that." Najid leaned forward and wiped her chin. "I'm only used to you responding to me like that."

Saadri opened her eyes in a playful giggle. A customer across the room met her eye and raised his glass in salute. Saadri arched a brow causing Najid to turn in the direction of her sight line. He nodded at the customer who then put money on the table and left the restaurant.

"Najid, you'd better finish your burger, you don't want it to get cold."

He turned toward his wife's voice and exclaimed, "You finished your half already?"

Saadri sheepishly held less than a quarter in her hand, "I still have some left." They laughed.

"Let's finish up so I can get you home." Saadri watched him attack his food without further conversation.

The warm cab was a welcomed respite from the dropping temperature. "Najid, I really enjoyed myself tonight, we have to do this more often."

He kissed her, "Yeah, I liked this too. We definitely have to get more of these types of nights in."

Saadri lay wrapped in her husband's arms, listening to his light snoring. The insistency of their lovemaking was more than enough to exhaust her energy but the sense that something was wrong kept her from sleeping. Najid's demeanor changed during the evening although he never changed his attentiveness. She prayed, again, for God to protect her husband. As much as she wanted him out of the streets, she knew he wasn't completely out.

Rasheen Raenier walked into Saadri's apartment with a smirk on his face. "So you called in the Calvary, huh?"

An exasperated Saadri blew a curl from the many that framed her face, teased upward from her scalp, and lay below her shoulders. "Your brother is out and about and he would have a fit if I went by myself so I called you. That girl is going to make me strangle her with this self-destructive crap. Then she has her best friend in the middle of all of this craziness too. I ought to call her mother to go get her! That would be a sight to see because Mon mon Nadine would kick Teran's behind all the way home! And she would deserve it!"

Rasheen inclined his head, "Now come on Dri, that's your sister. Sisters have to stick together. She's obviously letting off some steam. Let's go and get her."

Rasheen and Saadri walked into the Tilden Community Center and met a tall, slender young man. "Yo Rah! You looking for homegirl right? She is a cutie but she don't take no shorts! I had to let it be known she was off limits. Don't need Ace or Chris illin, you know what I mean?"

"Good looking out. Where is she, we'll scoop her up and book it." Rasheen took Saadri by the arm as they followed the young man to the back of the center where Teran and Fawn were seated among several young men who nodded when they saw Rasheen.

Saadri walked up her, "Sè, fé anler to-mèmm!"

Teran stood up as commanded, "Sè –"

"Fèrmé laboush!" Teran closed her mouth as Saadri scalded her with a look. "Lésé alé." Saadri grabbed her sister's arm and Fawn jumped up behind them.

Rasheen nodded to the young men and they left the party. Outside he questioned Fawn, "What happened?"

Fawn sighed, "She drank too much and I knew she was going to be hard to handle so I called Saadri. She is trying to forget her ex who left her a while back."

"How long is a while back?"

Fawn looked at Rasheen, awareness dawning, "It's going on nine months now."

Rasheen waved his arm and blew out a breath. "That's too long to be worrying over some dude. Terry is too pretty for that, and smart too. She needs someone to take her mind off of that punk."

Fawn raised an eyebrow but made no reply.

When they arrived at the house, Ellen was up and in the kitchen. "Bring the drunkie in here so we can get some coffee in her system. Saadri, call Nadine and let her know Teran is staying the night. Fawn, you call your parents too and we'll make sure you get home in the morning, right Rah?"

Rasheen helped Teran sit at the kitchen table, "Right Momma Ellen."

Saadri looked from Rasheen to her mother and they smiled knowingly. She then turned to Fawn, "Let's go in my room, I need to talk to you."

Chapter 14

Winter 1983

"Candy, are you going to pay attention to me or what?" Najid whispered and looked at his wife to ensure she understood his sentiment.

"Stop being so jealous, you always have my attention." She smiled at his rare petulance and kissed him. He pulled her closer for more.

Rasheen faced Teran, "What are you going to do once you graduate?"

"I'm getting out of here and going to college." She grinned as Rasheen grimaced. "I have to get an education."

With palms up he explained, "New York has some of the best schools in the country so why do you have to leave? Besides, we are just getting to know one another, I need more time with you. Are you going to make me travel a million hours to see you?"

"Would you travel to see me, if you had to?" Teran lowered her eyes then raised them.

"You know I would, I like you Terry. Why don't we see where this could go? I think we could be good together."

Teran wrinkled her nose as she smiled, "It just seems weird because we are family with your brother and my sister being together."

Rasheen nodded, "Yeah but that's not blood relations. It's not like we are kissing cousins or something. Let me show you." Rasheen approached the beautiful young woman in front of him and was happy she had not refused him.

Teran broke the kiss before Rasheen could intensify it. "My sister is across the table Rah."

He shrugged his shoulders, "So is my brother."

Teran grinned, "Yeah and he is probably cheering you on."

Najid laughed as he finished kissing Saadri, "You're right, I am cheering him on."

Saadri answered, "Now who's not paying attention? I feel neglected."

Najid turned toward her, "Stop lying girl, you don't feel neglected because I make sure you get plenty of attention."

They laughed and settled down to eat the meal brought to the table at Steve's Diner.

Saadri lay across her bed with Teran using her backside as a pillow; this was their favored position since childhood. Najid found them this way as he entered the room. "What are you twins up to?"

Saadri smiled as Teran answered, "Just enjoying one another's company. What are you up to?"

Najid removed his work shirt and laid it on the back of a chair. "I am going to go out for a while, I'll be back. You staying a while Terry? If you're here when I get back we'll walk you home."

Teran nodded her understanding of his veiled command as Saadri spoke, "Are you going to eat before you leave? Do you want me to leave something out for you?"

He walked over to the bed, covered Teran's eyes, and kissed his wife. Teran giggled, "I know you kiss your wife boy!"

He picked Teran up, "Who are you calling a boy? I know you see a man standing here."

"Najid stop before you drop her." Saadri left the bed and the room.

When Najid let Teran down she teased, "You are in trouble. She worries about you and you won't talk to her about what you are doing." He pushed her down on the bed. "Saadri! Najid is still bothering me!"

Saadri sat on the couch in the living room, Najid sat beside her. "When does Momma Ellie come out of the hospital?"

She laid her head on her husband's shoulder, "They are running more tests tomorrow. I am hoping by the end of the week because you know she doesn't want to be there. Najid –"

"I know baby. Everything will turn out just fine." He held her.

She took a breath and said what she held onto for a long while. "I am praying baby: for you, for us, for my mother, and for my sisters. I know you are into things you can't talk about. I know you're protecting me. I am asking God to protect you. I try to be strong but it is hard when so much happens all at once and I have to bear the weight. I need you but can't always have your undivided attention. I have always shared you with the streets and at times it's been as difficult and as hurtful as sharing you with another woman. Understand where I am in all of this Najid, I am suffering with you."

They looked at one another. "Candy, you never expressed yourself like this before. I just need more time baby to make sure we will be good, that everything will be good. Please hang on for me."

"I'm going upstairs to chill with Rasheen." Teran appeared in the living room.

"Don't lead my brother on. You're not over homeboy." Najid held Saadri as he spoke.

"No one is leading Rah on. We have talked and decided to remain good friends. Chill out." Teran huffed as she moved toward the door.

Saadri questioned, "Do you have a key?" Teran held it up and went out of the door.

"So Papa Damas is coming in when again?" Najid walked out of the living room, disrobing for his shower.

Saadri called, "He'll be here next week."

He stepped into the room clad in a towel wrapped around his waist. "Come take a shower with me Candy."

Shortly thereafter the evening took a turn and abruptly ended with Najid leaving in anger after they argued over whether to tell Damas they were married.

Ellen's cancer came back more aggressively and this time affected her kidneys, which caused her to need dialysis. She demanded Mary Clark come back as her on-call home attendant to the vexation of the family. Ellen and Saadri found themselves giving the men pep talks regarding their comportment around Mary. Damas took the lead as the family liaison with Mary as Saadri focused on keeping herself and Najid out of his path and line of questioning. As Damas scheduled to stay for a month, Saadri asked Najid to stay with his parents, which caused tension in the younger Raeniers undisclosed marriage.

Najid threw himself into his job and kept late hours. Further, he used the explanation of crowding in Saadri's apartment with Damas and Mary to stay away. Saadri ached for her husband's attention and felt badly for what she asked of him. Yet, part of her felt he asked equally much of her and she used this rationale to assuage her anxiety.

----------◊◊◊----------

Spring 84

Dialysis seemed to be helping Ellen a great deal as she became more vibrant, albeit, less active. She and Damas still danced around their relationship and Saadri still encouraged her mother to take the chance she denied herself for nearly twenty years. Ellen reminded Saadri to listen to her own advice as the latest argument centered on moving out of Brownsville and starting a family.

Najid walked into the apartment wearing a blue and white Adidas track suit and matching Adidas hat and sneakers. "Mrs. Raenier! Are you ready to hit it? We need to get up there by one."

Ellen walked into the hall as Najid walked toward the bedroom. "What are you yelling about this morning man?"

"Hey Momma Ellie." He wrapped his arms around her thin body and kissed her cheek. "Trying to get my wife to put a move on it, we need to be up in Harlem this afternoon and she knows the trains run slower on Saturdays." He made the last statement with his voice projecting toward the bedroom. Ellen laughed.

Saadri stepped out dressed in a loose fitting beige linen men's jacket once belonging to her father, a pair of black leggings and an orange and beige tunic. She topped it off with an orange scarf tied through her hair as a headband and a pair of orange pastel pointed toe heels. "You are loud enough without yelling directly into the room Najid. I told you I would be ready." She hoisted her beige and orange bucket bag onto her shoulder and walked toward the living room.

Najid watched her appreciatively and grabbed her, "Where are you trying to go, walking pass me without a hug or kiss?" He wrapped her in an embrace and scorched her lips with a kiss that led her to believe their struggle may have reached the truce stage.

She grinned. "I thought we had a train to catch?" Ellen laughed as her daughter hugged her.

"I am praying for good success for you two today. Mary is coming to help me do a few things so I will be in good hands." Ellen walked behind them to the front door.

Najid answered, "In that case, we won't be home for a while." Saadri pinched him and he looked at her as if she had two heads. "I am not spending my weekend dealing with that woman."

"Can't you be the bigger person?" Saadri pushed him toward the door.

"I am the bigger person and I am about to show you how much bigger if you keep pushing me wife. You know that woman and I can't stand to be around one another."

"Then it's best for you to stay gone a little while. I will have her out of here by six or seven this evening. To tell the truth I don't want to deal that long but she is good at what she does and good help is hard to find." Ellen patted Najid's shoulder. "Oh! While you're out, pick me up some French Coffee stockings for Teran's graduation. Y'all have all grown up. Nique finished her second year in school, you're married and moving out, and Terry is coming out of high school. Damas has no more babies; this is going to get good seeing him adjust to y'all as women. Is Terry going to Xavier?"

"Non Mon mon, she is staying here and going to Hunter. You know Pe'r gave her hell and I don't think it was right. She really wanted to go to California or Florida but he told her he wasn't paying for either and you know Mon mon Nadine didn't have that kind of money. Teran blew a scholarship too acting crazy. I personally think it's for the best that she stays here because she has been a loose cannon."

Ellen folded her arms and leaned against the open front door. Najid stepped into the hall and looked at his watch. "Isn't she better now, didn't you and Fawn convince her to stop all that mess?"

Saadri nodded, "Yeah, she stopped and I am glad. I will see you later Mon mon – my husband is getting impatient."

Najid massaged Saadri's shoulders, "We have to catch the train Candy. Plus I don't want Broom Hilda to fly in and ruin my morning."

Everyone laughed and Ellen waved them off, "Boy get out of here. You ought to stop. Take my child and go do what you are planning to do today." She closed the door still laughing.

The trains cooperated and Najid and Saadri were at the Lenox Avenue apartment building fifteen minutes before their appointment. Saadri looked at the 139th Street hi-rise and felt butterflies. The manager was friendly and joked with them all the way up to the eleventh floor where the vacant apartment they were interested in was located. He opened the door into a large living room with a balcony. Off to the left there was a galley, pass-through kitchen and an adjacent dining area. To the right of the living room was a hall that led to two bedrooms, one a master and the other a guest or additional bedroom. In the hall was a bathroom and there was another bathroom between the front door and the living room.

Saadri walked around excitedly thinking of how to decorate the space. "I want the house to have a theme with greens and golds. Ooh, we can paint the kitchen a bright, almost yellow color baby. Our bedroom can be a warm green with gold accents. The living room can be a brighter green because the light from the balcony will really accent it. The bathrooms will be easiest to decorate so we can start with those and our bedroom."

Najid watched her with pride. "Whatever you want to do Candy, that's fine with me. I'll make it happen." Najid turned to speak with the manager and caught a nuance that caused his blood to ice in his veins. He nodded.

The manager gave a nod, "Shall we go downstairs and talk business Mr. Raenier?"

Najid took his wife's hand, "Let's hit it baby."

Saadri was baffled and perturbed as she sat holding Najid's hand on the train. She didn't want to nag; she just wanted the courtesy of answers. "Would you please tell me why we rushed out of the house, to come all the way up here, to get excited about the place, to not take it? What caused the sudden change of mind? You went from telling me I could get whatever I wanted to practically dragging me away from the building."

Najid exhaled. He was caught in a game of cat and mouse and although he didn't like it, he was powerless to change the rules. His primary focus was his wife's safety. "Candy, let's talk about this at home." She huffed and said no more.

The torturous train ride over, Saadri descended the Rockaway Ave. staircase with purpose. Najid caught up to and grabbed her hand, she tried not to take it but he would have none of it. "I asked you to wait until we get home and we would talk about this."

"I am not going home."

"What?"

"I'm going to my sister's house." They hit the bottom step and Saadri made to cross the street but Najid thwarted her progress.

"Candy, let's go home and talk." He stared at her and she understood him completely.

She raised her chin, "I am going to my sister's house and we are going shopping."

The raised brow over Najid's left eye demonstrated his shock at her response. He leaned in closer and whispered in her ear. "I don't want a scene out here and everybody in our business. Let's just go home and iron this out."

Saadri looked at him and smiled, "No darling, I am going to my sister's house and then I am going shopping. At least I gave you the respect of communicating my reasoning and whereabouts." She removed her hands and stepped around him. "Don't wait up."

Teran's graduation and Damas' arrival at the apartment placed the Raenier deadlock on pause. Najid again became scarce as Saadri chose not to focus on him but to celebrate her sister's accomplishment. Veronique came up for the special day with the understanding that she would leave soon after to attend summer classes.

Chapter 15

Damas sat at the head of special seating the Arcadia staff created for his family. To his right sat Ellen, Saadri, Mazie -his mother, and Veronique. To his left were Teran, Nadine, and Nadine's children Ayana and Talib, and Nadine's mother, Margie Jackson. Gordon Jackson sat at the other end of the table facing Damas.

Gordon looked at Damas, "Boy, who you know to get us in this place and it's brand new?"

Damas raised his arms in a gesture of faux innocence. "Well you know, Gordon, I do travel around a bit. I'm a business man."

Gordon nodded, "Oh, that's what they call it!" The sisters laughed aloud, Ellen hid her smirk, Mazie nodded demurely, and Margie exhaled.

"Daddy you and Damas are not starting that today. This is for Teran." Nadine looked from one man to the other and both shrank back into their seats.

Damas muttered, "Someone woke the Kracken."

Nadine bit out, "DO NOT start in here boy." Teran, Ayana, and Talib snickered until Nadine turned a look of censure in their direction.

Damas spoke aloud, "This is Teran's day so your reign of terror is on a cease-fire Nadine."

Ellen spoke, "Damas stop it. You always start and try to make Nadine look like the bad guy." Mazie motioned for Damas to stop and he clamped down on the response he had ready.

Gordon took his place, "For the life of me I don't know how he and Nadine shut up long enough to have Teran; probably fought through that too."

The sisters, Ayana, and Talib lost composure as Margie turned toward Gordon. The look she gave him could melt wax. Gordon raised his shoulders, "It's an honest observation." Uncontained, uncontrollable laughter ensued before servers came to the table with a family style meal that garnered the attention of all.

After the celebratory lunch, Gordon invited everyone back to the Jackson's downtown Brooklyn brownstone for continued festivities. Damas spoke for all as he loaded his rental car for Clinton Hill. The sisters and Ayana took a leisurely stroll across the city to the Columbus Avenue train station.

Veronique smiled at her youngest sister, "I cannot believe the brat is finished with high school! So why aren't you coming to North Carolina so we can all be together?"

"I am not a brat!" Teran's hand on her hip, she playfully rolled her eyes.

"Yes you are and I am here to tell you!" Ayana asserted with a finger point. Veronique and Saadri burst into laughter.

Saadri hugged Ayana, "Poor baby didn't get a chance to be spoiled with Terry around. You really should have been the oldest daughter."

"Later for all of you! I am the oldest and that's final. I can't go with you and Saadri because I have a job. I start next week."

Veronique raised her eyebrows. "You got a job? Good for you! Why are you starting so close to graduation?"

Teran folded her arms as she looked down the tracks for sign of an incoming train. "I am saving my money and getting out of Nadine's house as fast as possible."

"Are things that bad Terry?" Saadri stepped closer. "You can stay with us if you'd like."

"She can't leave me with the Dragon Lady. She needs to wait for me to get out at least, especially if my father keeps rolling in and out." Ayana visibly shook.

Veronique waved an arm, "Well, you owe me a visit then, Terry. What are you doing this summer?"

The train moved into the station and the four ladies sat on a bench that would accommodate them all. They made a point of ignoring looks of interest from other riders. As they settled, Teran responded. "I will be a college aide at the Municipal Building here in Manhattan. It pays well and I should be able to have a nice looking bank account by the end of the summer. Who knows, maybe I can get Fawn to move out with me. She doesn't work that far from me. Anyway, that's my plan. I have to be a big girl now." She grabbed Ayana's hand and smiled reassuringly.

"I didn't hear anything about school. What are your plans since you escaped the Xavier noose?" Veronique threw a pointed look in Saadri's direction. "It's bad enough Saadri didn't go, I don't want you doing the same thing."

With a shake of her head, Saadri engaged, "Everyone sitting here knows what a rollercoaster my life has been of late with my mother being sick. I will get to school; it's just on hold for now. You can be so-"

Teran added, "Like Merci! Whether we step foot on an HBCU campus or not, we still are your sisters and our lives will still have value-"

Veronique scalded them with a look, "You know doggone well I am not saying that so don't go there! I want to see the two of you excel because I know you can."

"You mean you want us to get out of the projects." Teran rolled her eyes.

Veronique gave her a nudge, "Yes! I will not apologize for wanting that for both of you. For you too Ayana so listen carefully. There's a great, big world out there and you won't see it from the projects. No slight to Mon mon Ellie or Mon mon Nadine because they have raised three intelligent young women. I just want you to go out and explore the world and see what you could have."

Ayana touched Veronique's arm, "I understand what you mean and I know they do too. You know how your Doublemint sisters team up and gang up on everybody." Teran looked at her sister as if she mortally wounded her. Ayana waved the reaction away. Saadri looked at the exchange and shook her head. Ayana continued, "You see Nique? That's what I mean. Teran is the Drama Queen and Saadri is the Martyr."

Veronique howled. "She has you two down pat! Thank you Yana, I have had to deal with those two all my life and it's not been easy."

Saadri jerked, "Not easy for who? We haven't been a lot of trouble for you because you always saved your own butt by running back and telling on us."

Teran touched Saadri's arm, "Don't forget how she would pinch us before she ran to tell. So bossy, we couldn't do anything." Saadri nodded.

Green eyes blazed in expanded orbs, "I had to pinch you because then you knew I meant business. And yes, I had to run and tell because as the oldest I would get into more trouble if I didn't. I couldn't breathe for having to watch what the two of you imps were getting into next."

Ayana laughed as she listened to the exchange. "Now look at you, three women, three beautiful women. You are handling life and staying close, MY three big sisters."

Veronique placed an arm around her shoulders, "It's alright Yana, you can tell them that I am your favorite sister."

Saadri and Teran pushed her as Ayana laughed. "Nique you are Big Mama, when you speak I listen and follow directions. Saadri and Teran are the two angels that sit on your shoulder - one good and one that gets you into trouble."

The three sisters looked at Teran and said, "We know who the trouble angel is."

"Oh so we are ranking now, on my graduation day? Okay. I see how y'all are. I may be the one who gets you into trouble but I am the one who lives, I go out and do things." Teran sat back with a pout.

"You throw tantrums too, don't forget that." Saadri bumped against her, causing Teran to laugh. "For the record, I get out too." Teran gave her an incredulous look to which Saadri waved her away.

Veronique harrumphed at the statement, "Where do you go Saadri? You're watched like a hawk by a bulldog. I'm surprised you're even coming with me; your Hard Rock didn't have anything to say about it? He is actually letting you leave his sight for more than twenty-four hours?"

Teran looked at Saadri, "How long are you staying with Nique?"

Saadri smiled, "A month, I come back the end of July or early August."

Teran formed an 'o' with her mouth. "You're staying that long? Najid is going for that?"

"He is not my-" Saadri thought better of the wording. "Keeper or Lord and Master. I told him I was leaving for a month and there is nothing he can do about it. We need the space."

"Trouble in paradise? Who would have thought?" Veronique watched Saadri with a raised eyebrow.

"Cut it out Merci!" Teran threw Veronique a look of challenge. "You may not like Najid but he's Saadri's man. She loves him."

"I never said I don't like Najid." Veronique placed a hand on her chest.

Saadri shook her head, "She couldn't because she would be lying but I know she doesn't think he is good enough for me. That class thing runs deep with Miss St. Amant."

Teran sucked her teeth, "Yeah, you know she slums it whenever she is with us. We only get the privilege of seeing her because she's our sister."

Veronique's face contorted, "Oh gag me with a spoon!" The foursome broke into a fit of laughter.

Chris Hanley was waiting beneath the tracks of the Livonia Street train station when Najid arrived. The two walked toward one another and leaned against adjacent sides of a support column. Chris started the conversation, "To tell the truth I was surprised about this consulting thing. You out or what?"

Najid looked at the Van Dyke buildings within his line of vision. "It's all relative man, you know that."

Chris nodded, "Yeah, I'm learning more as the days go by. So how do we get this done?"

"It's a process man; we get it done over a few weeks." For the first time Najid was thankful for Saadri's extended absence.

October 1984

"Man, get out of the mirror! You don't need anything trimmed because everything is legit."

"Thanks Rah." Najid looked at the newly attached beard, goatee, and mustache with appreciation, it made him look stable and established. Yet, he was far from either. The summer brought several "consults" and things between he and Saadri became rockier as they argued over everything from the match of wills with Mary to starting a family. He watched his reflection and wondered how long he'd be on a string; he knew not to relax or believe anyone had forgotten. Too many messages were sent to remind him that his presence meant a disruption of business. It was only a matter of time. He grunted, grateful for the stretch that allowed him to put things in place for Saadri.

"So is Teran going to the wedding?"

He turned toward Rasheen, "She's the maid-of-honor." There was no need to remind him that he doubted the two had a real chance at a relationship since she and the ex-boyfriend had made up. "Yo Rah-"

"I know she's back with homeboy. He'd better make her happy or I'm taking him out." Rasheen walked away from the bathroom. Najid closed the door to take his shower.

"I never knew Hard Rocks could clean up so well!" Veronique admired the cut of the brown striped suit. "This is a bad suit Najid!"

He admired the black, pink and green panel dress that hugged Veronique's curves and ended at her knees. The dress had a short black jacket with shoulder pads that complemented the symmetrical pattern of the dress. She paired them with three-inch T-strap spiked heeled shoes in matching black, pink, and green. The natural golden highlights of her hair sparked within the curls that framed her face and fell down her back. She teased the hair and added spray to maintain the desired height; black thunderbolt earrings peaked from under the hair. She was at six feet with her shoes on. "Nique, you look like a model. I hope I won't have to break someone's neck tonight over you." He kissed her cheek.

She laughed, "We Buard girls know how to handle ourselves. Wait until you see your woman."

Najid bristled internally; he was tired of being a secret. Then again, the way things had been of late, and especially between them, he figured he would just have to settle with it for the time being. He inhaled. Saadri walked toward him in a brown, pink, and yellow fitted floral polyester dress with long sleeves that softly ruffled mid-forearm, the hem held a soft ruffled flare that began at the knees and ended mid-calf. Caramel-chestnut brown leather vamps with high spiked heels and a ruched front tapering to a pointed toe completed the ensemble. "Candy."

Saadri heard him call her name in a breath and felt her insides liquefy. She smiled. It was the first genuinely tender moment between them in what seemed like ages. She walked into his outstretched arms and kissed him with a thirst she could no longer keep at bay. "You look so handsome baby."

Najid whispered, "Do we have to go to this wedding?"

Saadri giggled, "Absolutely! I spent some time getting this together and now I am going out to show it off so come on and don't give me any trouble."

She walked out of the embrace but he grabbed her back and whispered in her ear. "You're getting bossy Mrs. Raenier."

She whispered in return, "I learned from the best."

Fawn's wedding took place in a converted space in her parents' Crown Heights home. Several shades of silver entered the room before the darkest shade appeared. A nickel colored dress accentuated all of Teran's shapely beauty – modest bosom, curved waist, flat stomach, and round hips. All of the Buard girls were built in similar fashion although Saadri was the most petite of the three. Najid shook his head as he watched the youngest sister. "I'm going to have a headache tonight! I can't believe how she is wearing that dress! Looks like the thing wants to melt off her she's so hot." When a tall, dark, solidly built young man turned toward him he made eye contact. Their eyes communicated equal readiness to accept any challenge. The young man turned around.

"Sitoplé Najid! You are too loud Be." The young man again turned in the direction of the voice and staggered as he looked into Saadri's face. A snicker at the couple drew his attention to the beige face of a blond and light brown haired bombshell that brought back the term brick house. A light of recognition dawned. He smirked and turned to watch Teran.

Fawn arrived in a halo of sun that caused the room to gasp in appreciation. Reggie, her groom, proudly stepped forward to receive his fiancé from her father. Teran positioned herself at an angle with the rest of the bridesmaids and the view of her alluring profile and flawless feet in a pair of matching nickel pumps was arresting. Najid groaned again, "Good grief all y'all got them curves!"

When the same young man turned, they stared off. Najid nodded his head toward the exit but Saadri spoke to him as she witnessed the exchange. "Najid arété please. You are such a trip!"

The blonde bombshell chimed in with, "Be quiet Hood Rat and stop talking so loud." They snickered and settled down.

Chapter 16

The ceremony was short and simple. Everyone cheered for the groom as he kissed his new bride, even Najid gave an encouraging, "Yeah boy!" The guests moved down into the basement where tables were arranged indoors and in the back yard under a tent ready with heaters for the unpredictable October weather. Outside there were two food tables filled with delicacies, a portable bar, and a small dance area.

The threesome entered the yard and Veronique asked, "Where should we sit?"

Najid watched the young man from upstairs approach and spoke to Saadri, "Hey Candy you and your sister step away a minute. I might have to check this clown once and for all."

Saadri warned, "Najid he is a pretty big guy and you are not going to ruin this wedding with this stuff. Both of you were staring at one another and both of you shouldn't have been at someone else's affair acting like that. Come on now, please don't start out here." Najid looked at Saadri and she became silent and lowered her eyes.

Veronique voiced concern, "Don't shut her down like that! She's right and you'd better not act fool out here tonight."

The young man stood before the small group and in a thick Jamaican accent greeted. "Mi name ah Bashan but mi go by Shan an Teran mi ooman. Dat wud mek yuh all mi fambily cuz wi marry soon."

"Bashan!" Saadri squealed and grabbed him about the waist. He hugged her in return. Veronique joined their embrace with a bright smile.

Bashan looked at Saadri. "Yuh affi be de twin cuz yuh duh luk laik Teran suh much." He then looked at Veronique, "An yuh de oldest sista live inna North Carolina. Yuh all suh pretty."

Najid nodded in recognition, "So you're homeboy. I'm Najid and you are all over my woman. What's up man?" He extended his hand to Bashan and they dapped as Najid looked at Saadri by the tall man's side.

Veronique joked, "She was welcoming him to the family; he is not trying to take her!" Najid shot a look toward Veronique and she rolled her eyes.

Bashan laughed, "Gud fi meet yuh all. Teran tole mi bout yuh an mi glad yuh here at de wedding. Najid here yuh ooman!" They shared a laugh. "Mi possessive ova Teran too."

Saadri and Veronique chimed, "Yeah, we heard." Bashan frowned and they laughed.

Bashan led them to the table where another woman was seated. The wedding party was upstairs taking pictures. Calypso started playing and the fourth woman stood, her Cabotine de Gres perfume emanating from her pulse points. "Okay Shan you must dance with me." She pulled him from the table as Veronique and Saadri looked on.

"Now it's my turn and I'm telling you don't nut at this wedding." Najid leaned in close to Saadri's ear.

Saadri shook her head, "Real funny. But that's my sister's man and homegirl is acting like she owns him."

"Don't worry, this will be her only dance with him and she is finding somewhere else to sit." Veronique was about to get up from the table when Najid's hand stilled her. She shot him a warning look he paid no attention to.

"Sit down Nique. He's a big boy and he knows how to put her in her place. Let it play out and you will find out all you need to know." Najid looked at her until she sat.

"How do you do that?" Veronique sat with a thump.

"Do what?" Najid sat back in his seat and put his arm around Saadri.

"You speak without speaking."

Najid shook his head while Saadri answered, "Girl I've been trying to figure that out forever."

Veronique watched as the woman, Andrea, began to dance closer to Bashan. Then everyone's attention was diverted to the entrance of the wedding party. Three bridesmaids, both sets of parents, the best man, and Teran entered before Reggie and Fawn. They waved at Teran who smiled brightly.

As the dancers walked back to the table Veronique gave Saadri a signal to follow her lead; she gave her sister a slight shove and Saadri opened a seat for Bashan. "Well brother dear, you must sit and talk with us." Veronique grabbed Bashan's arm and led him to the seat next to her. They sat and Saadri sat on the opposite side of Bashan. Andrea moved to the other side of the table. Najid shook his head when he saw what happened and held out a chair for the stranded woman. He ignored the daggers his wife aimed in his direction. He did his best to keep her engaged in the table conversation.

After a while of partying, the guests assembled on the main floor to see the newlyweds off on their honeymoon. When they descended from the second floor where they changed, confetti flew into the air. Bashan led an inebriated, ego-bruised Andrea out of the door to his car. He did not realize Teran spotted him or that through the windshield she could make out a female.

"Éou zòt tô bo va, Sè" Veronique spoke behind Teran.

"If I knew where he was going, we would both be inside instead of out here with me mad as hell!" Teran turned to walk inside.

Veronique took her by the arm, "Then why not go to the car and ask him where he is going rather than stand here yelling at me for asking the question. I am with you. We can pull that heifer out of the car and teach her a lesson Buard style.

Teran joked, "Shaer, you're a St. Amant."

Veronique laughed, "Oh yes, an illustrious St. Amant. Mercy, mercy me!"

"No Shaer, Merci on us all!"

"Hey, stop talking about my mother. Mon mon Nadine is no walk in the park!" Veronique placed a manicured hand on her hip.

"Why are you two out here? Everything okay?" Saadri knit her brows together.

"How did you get out here without your bodyguard?" Veronique jibed. Teran burst into laughter.

"Oh so you two got jokes now? Where is your big Jamaican, Terry? He's a cutie, I liked him right off. Granmè know about him? Does Pe'r know about him? He said you two were getting married? Is that true? I know I'd better be in my twin's wedding! Later for Nique and Yana, I know I'm your favorite sister. What will your colors be? How does Mon mon Nadine like him? I know Yana has something to say, I'm going to get her for not calling me and telling me – What?"

Teran and Veronique stood silently watching Saadri; Veronique spoke, "How in the world can you ask so many questions and not let a person get in one answer? Good grief, where's the fire?"

Teran nudged Veronique, "You know she has to get it all in while she's not with Bruiser. He shuts it all down when he comes on the scene." The sisters laughed again at Saadri's expense. When they saw they may have wounded her they stopped. "Dri we are just kidding. We both love Najid with his fine self. He's a Hard Rock for sure but he loves you and we know he treats you well. That's all we can ask for. Have you two thought about marriage?" Saadri looked pained. "Dri? What's the matter Sè?"

"Umm, I have to tell you something. We … uh... Najid and I … well…" The sisters looked at one another before looking at Saadri as if to say 'out with it!' "Okay, here it is – we got married at the justice of the peace over the summer."

"What?!" The two chorused before Veronique spoke up.

"When you got back from North Carolina?" Teran questioned.

Saadri bit her lip, "No Sè, last summer."

Veronique threw her arms in the air, "You have been married a whole year and we knew nothing about it? So when were you planning to tell us?"

Teran choked out, "You didn't tell me Saadri?" Saadri touched her arm.

Veronique queried, "He is your husband – ooh, does Pe'r know?" Saadri shook her head. "Granmè?' Saadri shook again. "Oh crap Dri, you've done it now."

"What did she do?" Najid walked up to the threesome.

Teran went to embrace him, "Well my cutie Hard Rock, it seems congratulations are in order because you're now my bofrè, my brother-in-law." She kissed his cheek.

"Thanks gorgeous, I am happy to be part of the family. Now I have three beauties to protect. When Nique came up the last time, it was a headache but I managed it."

Veronique pushed Najid who grabbed her and kissed her on the cheek. "Let me go you ruffian! Wait, you guys got married last summer! Before or after I came?"

Najid looked at Saadri and held out his hand. She came to him. "We tied the knot after Saadri graduated, literally, on that day."

Veronique shook her head, "Ya'll are a piece of work! Wait until Pe'r finds out Dri. He's going to have a fit. Can I tell my mother?"

Saadri and Teran responded, "Non!"

"Ya'll better stop talking about my mother!" All of the sisters laughed.

Najid asked, "What's wrong with Nique's mother?"

Teran quipped, "Just wait until you meet Merci." She smirked and sent a covert look toward Veronique who rolled her eyes. They all went inside to help with clean up.

When the doorbell rang an hour later the threesome gave covert acknowledgements of Teran's displeasure. They watched Bashan enter the living room. "Hey Miss, mi kno yuh ah vex but please yuh nuffi cah mi ena dween a gud deed."

Najid asked Saadri, "What did he just say? She can understand him?" Saadri nudged him. He spoke to Bashan. "You know she's pissed and she should be. You cut out on her and she didn't know where you were, what's up with that? I'm glad we were here to wait with her."

Teran offered, "Shan, Saadri and Najid are married so you're talking to my brother-in-law. You two will have to get along so don't start acting crazy in here."

"Laik yuh an fi mi mudda rite Teran?" Bashan snorted in Teran's direction.

Saadri took the opportunity to break the ice. "Oh Lord Terry, you have a Merci?"

Veronique volleyed, "Non she has a Nadine and that's bad enough. We can't all be Saint Ellens."

"Ooh! So we are ranking now?!" Teran became animated.

The sisters looked at one another and exclaimed, "It's on!"

Bashan turned to Najid, "Ah dey laik dis aal de while? Dey chime inna lacka chorus - dree blind mice!"

"Oh sweat, three blind mice! Ha! I have to get used to your accent but that was good man." Najid nodded toward Bashan.

"Don't start you two because we can have a session!" Veronique challenged.

Najid answered with, "Why are you always the ring leader? Do you have a man? You have so much mouth, and I thought Candy had mouth!"

Bashan added, "Teran ah nuh slouch, shi ave much mout!"

Teran added, "Yeah I do and this mouth is getting ready to go off on you. Who was in your car and why were they in your car?"

"Teran mi took Andrea home. Shi drank a likkle too much an mi nuh waan har pon de train laik dat."

Saadri pounced. "Put the heifer in a cab! You aint her man! You got my sister here waiting for you and all nasty with us while you trying to play the gentleman with some skeezer!" Najid wrapped his arms around her waist and whispered in her ear.

Veronique was about to speak but Najid intercepted. "Nique, let's get our stuff and let these two handle their business. Come let me talk to you about finding you a good man to keep you preoccupied and calm you down." He laughed when he said the last part as she was baited.

"I don't need you to find a man for me and I am not interested in one of your Hood Rat friends." She walked with Saadri and Najid into another room.

Bashan playfully pinched Teran and she rolled her eyes. "Yuh ah almost reddi fi guh?"

"What about my family? They will need a ride home, they live in Brownsville too." She went up to Fawn's room to gather her things.

Bashan followed the path the others took and found them lounging in the den. "Yuh ah reddi fi lef fambily? Najid point mi inna de rite direction an mi will tek yuh home."

Najid stood and helped Saadri out of her seat. "You got it Bro-in-law. Come on baby. We are going home. Big Mouth you get up and come on too." Veronique sucked her teeth and stood.

"Mi cyan get ova ou yuh luk just laik fi mi babi. Mi luk pon yuh an mi see Teran." Bashan shook his head in disbelief.

"Well make no mistake, this one here is my Candy. Besides, she's older so Terry looks like her! But we both have good taste because all of them are fine!"

"Dem ah fine indeed." Bashan dapped Najid as Teran walked into the den.

"Is everyone ready?" She looked at the men, "Glad to see the testosterone contest is over." She turned and walked toward the front door.

Veronique walked up to Bashan, "Ohh are you in trouble Big Boy! Terry is pissed. Let's see you take another hussy home."

"Mouth Almighty, please mind your own business! The man don't need you stirring up trouble between him and his woman." Najid steered Saadri out of the den. He looked back and saw Veronique standing there, grabbed her hand, then yanked, "Let's go woman before I drag you out of here by your hair. Then you can add Cave Man to the list of names you call me."

Bashan laughed aloud, "Dat wud be a sight fi mi yeye fi see!"

Veronique had a retort ready. "Cool it Reggae Boy! You aint in the family yet!"

Bashan snorted, "Oh mi am inna de fambily arite. Mi see de mout runs drough de sistas."

Najid pulled Veronique, "Yes it does, this is one trait I can do without. As pretty as they are, is as much mouth as they bring!"

"Najid stop talking about my sisters. Obviously we need the mouth to deal with you two apes!" Saadri continued walking.

Najid lowered his voice, "Don't worry, I know how to shut that mouth."

Bashan howled, "Mi ave de siem crosses wid Teran. Shi rises up den mi affi show har ooo de mon."

Saadri and Veronique yelled, "Terry!"

Teran was on the outside landing when she heard them call. "What's going on? Come out of these folks' house making all that noise!"

They said their goodbyes to the Welches and filed out the front door. The drama commenced on the block and a half walk to Bashan's car.

Saadri was by Teran's side. "So Shan shows you who the man is 'cause that's what he said?"

Veronique agreed, "Bashan and Hard Rock said we have too much mouth and Najid said he knows how to shut Dri's mouth."

Saadri sucked her teeth. "Ki fé pensé-yé nouzòt to?"

Najid jumped in front of the women. "Time! First of all I had no idea you could speak another language and second say everything in English so we can understand. I have a tough enough time following my man here."

Bashan placed a hand over his heart. "Mi dought wi were pon de siem side Najid." He sucked his teeth mimicking Saadri. The group laughed.

Saadri answered with, "You are trying to go to war Shan. I said for those who didn't know- who did the two of you think we were."

Bashan put both hands in the air. "Sup'm tells mi wi ago find out." They all laughed as they arrived at the car.

Teran sat in the front seat at Najid's insistence. They settled in and Teran questioned, "Shan who was the chick and why did she stick up under you tonight? She didn't even want me to dance with you!"

"T shi Reggie's coworka an wi met tenight."

"Tonight and you driving her home?! Let me just meet someone and go off with them and it's World War Six but you go off and don't know her from Eve."

"Mi ena trying fi be a gentleman, mi kno yuh wud be bizzy wid de reception an de newlyweds suh mi took har home an cum rite bak here fi yuh. Besides mi kno yuh had fi yuh sistas an Najid. Nutten went pon or wud guh pon cah yuh ah de ongle ooman mi luv T. Be gud fi Daddy an don't quarrel wid mi babi. Mi waan taak bout dat dress yuh had pon yuh badi."

Najid cut in, "He wants to talk about getting you out of that dress and I don't blame him 'cause you wore the stitches out of it!"

"Najid!" Saadri covered her mouth while Veronique shrieked.

"What?! Candy if you had worn a dress like that I would have stopped the wedding, 'Pardon me everyone but I got to take this gift home and unwrap the package'!" The car erupted.

Bashan reached over and caressed Teran's thigh. "See im undastan mi. Nuhbadi lukked laik yuh did inna dat dress. Wah mek mi wud waan sum oda ooman wen mi ave yuh? Mi luv yuh gyal."

Saadri gushed, "I am so glad my sister has your devotion. Welcome to the family."

Najid chimed in, "Welcome to the family man. It's good to have a brother to help out with this trio, they are a handful. We have to do some things together."

Three sets of eyes focused on Veronique. Bashan watched her from the rearview mirror. She huddled in a corner and stared out the window. Najid reached behind Saadri and placed a hand on her shoulder, "You okay Nique?"

"I'm proud of my sisters, welcome to you both." She sighed and continued to watch the passing sights.

Chapter 17

Saadri picked up the phone with butterflies in her stomach and was relieved to hear Teran on the other end. They didn't speak long. "Pe'r is coming Terry and he's pissed."

Ellen Weston opened the door to her apartment and looked into the eyes of Nadine Scott. She inhaled, "Y'all come on in. Saadri told me she and her twin were up to it again but this is a big one." They entered the apartment and Nadine wanted to embrace the frail woman but she knew it would never be welcomed. Ellen pointed toward her couch, "Have a seat. Can I get you anything? Dri! Your twin is here."

They sat and Teran asked, "Where's Najid?"

Ellen shook her head, "Who knows? He is a bit of a phantom around here."

Saadri entered the living room and signaled for Teran to end the line of conversation. Teran asked, "Mon mon Ellen, can I get some iced tea or something?"

Ellen sat at her kitchen table, "You know you are welcomed to get what you need. Go ahead and make sure you get some for your momma."

Nadine got Saadri's attention to thwart any conspiring between her and her sister. "Dri, can you please tell me how you forgot to tell your father you were married? I know he is one crazy Creole by now. How did he find out?"

Ellen chimed in, "How else?"

They looked at one another and said, "Merci."

Teran handed her mother a glass of tea and spoke, "Nique didn't do it on purpose. She didn't know Dri still hadn't told Pe'r. She only told us at Fawn's wedding."

Ellen laughed, "They stick up for one another don't they Nay."

Nadine was jolted; it had been a long time since she heard Ellen use the nickname. She swallowed more tea and responded, "I know Ellie, and we have Miss Mazie to thank for making sure they grew up together. Now we have to keep Damas from coming up here and causing havoc."

Saadri and Teran sat next to one another on dining room chairs. Both mothers looked at them and laughed. Ellen remarked, "Remember that picture of them when they were about two? They were all hugged up and smiling like they were little angels when they had just finished getting into mischief. Looked like little Indian babies or something. Now they are sitting there trying to look pitiful and helpless."

Nadine responded, "Yeah I know. They want me to go toe-to-toe with Damas for them. This is their mess!"

"Well." Ellen shrugged her shoulders.

"Not you too Ellie, why me?" Nadine drained her tea and held the cup out for Teran who retrieved more for her, "Just a little more Teran."

Ellen shifted in her seat. "You know full well you are the only who can go toe-to-toe with him. You give as good as you get. He always bullied Merci and me, well, you know me."

"Yeah Ellie, I get it. Let the Queen B handle it. I know." Nadine also shifted in her seat. "I have to get my head ready for him. You know he is a ball breaker."

Saadri went over to Nadine and hugged her. "Thank you so much Mon Mon Nay. I just can't do all of that and I sure don't want Pe'r and Najid to lock horns."

Teran and Ellen both echoed, "Oh no!"

"I say let it be the clash of the Titans and may the best man win," Nadine laughed.

Saadri looked grief stricken and Teran stood by her. "Ma stop, you know that wouldn't be anything but disastrous."

Nadine kept laughing, "Oh and then I'd let him loose on the Big Jamaican and really see the sparks fly!" Ellen joined in the laughter as the sisters watched helplessly. The longer they stood looking horrified the more the two women laughed.

Catching a breath Ellen reflected, "You always were a trip Nay. It's never a dull moment with you!"

"I miss you too Ellie." Nadine lowered her eyes.

The room went silent before Saadri spoke. "Maybe there are some other things that need to be said before Pe'r gets here. We are going up to see the Raeniers. We'll be back later." She ushered Saadri out of the door.

Ellen looked at Nadine and sighed, "It is about that time, isn't it?"

Nadine nodded, "Long overdue."

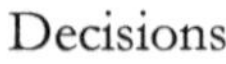

Early November 1984

Damas Buard caused a quiet disturbance at LaGuardia Airport as onlookers debated whether he was Howard Hewitt or Smokey Robinson. Used to the attention his appearance garnered he headed, undistracted, for the car rental counter. The shapely customer service agent gratuitously upgraded his vehicle and offered perks he just winked at. Damas was on a mission. He knew his girls well enough to know they had a strategy for dealing with his arrival but they didn't know he had a counter for their defense. Once settled in the car he mentally mapped his itinerary.

Nadine looked out her peephole and quietly chided, "No he didn't!" She opened the door and Damas Buard stood on the other side with his mother, Mazie. "I had no idea when you would come. Come on in."

He kissed her cheek, "Bonjou, aou Teran?"

Nadine hugged Mazie, "Bonjou Mon mon. It's so good to see you; it's been a long time." Mazie walked into the apartment and Nadine pointed toward the kitchen – she knew it was the room the older woman preferred. Damas stood next to her. "Teran is not here right now, I will call for her to come home."

"Where is she?" Damas touched Nadine's arm to stop her progress.

Nadine audibly exhaled, "She is in Queens with her fiancé; they have an apartment."

"You let her move in with him?"

"No Damas. She won't move in until after the wedding." Nadine walked into the kitchen with him hot on her heels.

"She may as well if she stays there all night like they are already married."

Nadine dialed.

"I didn't expect her to be up here playing house!"

She listened as the phone rang.

"What is going on up here with mo fiy running around like loose cannons?"

Bashan picked up and she began without ceremony. "I need you and Teran to get out here right away. As you can hear, her father is here."

Teran unlocked the door to the Brownsville apartment an hour later and was met with, "Bonjou fiy. Konmen ça va?"

"Bonjou Pe'r. Çé bon." She walked into her father's arms and kissed his cheek. Bashan walked in behind her, "Pe'r this is Bashan, he has been waiting to meet to you."

Damas raised a brow, "Really? Why have we not met then mo shou?"

Teran inhaled, "It was my fault, I kept waiting and before I knew it here we are -" The look he gave her stopped her words.

Damas extended a hand, "I am pleased to finally meet you Bashan. From the look of my daughter I owe her happiness to you. I would like to talk, man-to-man, you know?"

Bashan smiled and met his handshake. "Mi wud be happy fi taak wid yuh Mista Buard. Mi am very glad fi be finally meeting yuh."

"Mo fé tendé mâ mo tit-fiy?" (Is that my granddaughter I hear?) An attractive, petite, fair, older woman appeared in the hall.

Teran gasped, "Granmè! Bonjou!" She turned to her father, "Pe'r you didn't say you were bringing Granmè with you." The look on Damas' face let Teran know he'd meant to leave that bit of information out. She groaned inwardly but reached for Bashan's hand. "Granmè, çe mâ bo, Bashan." She brought Bashan to stand in front of Mazie and coached him to say hello.

Mazie watched the tall young man in front of her for a moment before smiling and embracing him. "Bonjou, pleased to meet you."

"Granmè you are speaking English now?"

"For him shaer, wi."

They all walked into the living room to meet Ellen, Saadri, Najid, and Nadine. Teran commented, "The gang's all here I see."

Saadri answered, "Bonjou Sè. Come sit by me. Hi Bashan." Saadri held out her arms and Bashan walked into her embrace before giving Najid some dap.

Najid spoke into Bashan's hearing, "Old Man's a trip and he has these girls on lockdown. We gonna have to step up to the plate with him or he will try to punk us out for real."

Bashan nodded, "Gat fi yuh bak; wi ah nuh guh out laik dat."

Najid grinned, "My man," and clapped him on the back. They resettled on the couch with the sisters between them.

Mazie looked at the foursome and smiled, "Tou mâ ti piti."

Saadri interpreted softly, "She likes you two; she called you her little children." She looked up into her father's green storm clouds.

Damas folded his arms and bore down. "I am not a man to beat around the bush. I am more than ticked with this whole situation. My daughters are up here running wild and I hear about things after they have happened. Are one or both of you pregnant?"

Nadine sucked her teeth, "You know you are about as subtle as a Mack truck!"

He glared at Nadine, "And you are letting Teran run around here like the original Wild Woman of Borneo! At least Saadri is married!"

Teran lowered her head and Bashan tensed but Nadine volleyed. "Our daughter has done nothing to be ashamed of, she is not being wild."

"She just spent the night out and came in with him and I am supposed to be happy that my daughter is playing house?!"

"Sah wi ah getting marrid inna de spring. Wi ah working an saving fi de wedding now." Bashan's movements were hindered by the weight of Teran's deflated body.

Damas pointed at Bashan, "You are telling me, you didn't ask me like a gentleman for my daughter's hand! Just like that one just took my daughter like I didn't matter."

"Mr. Buard I love your daughter and I wanted to make a commitment to her to show her how much I love her." Najid wanted to stand but Saadri wrapped her arms around his waist. Her rapid heartbeat angered him.

Damas looked from Najid to Bashan. "I am not an absent parent. Those are my babies and I should have been informed all the way. This is not what I expected and I am not about to come up here and act like everything is okay because it's not!"

"Mo shagrin Pe'r" Teran rasped out before she broke into a sob. Bashan held his breath to keep from exploding as he comforted her.
"Mo …. shagrin," Saadri broke as she spoke and Najid consoled her, thankful for the diversion.

"Damas you've made them cry." Ellen was near tears.

Nadine fired, "You come in kicking butt and taking names but you don't stop to see what's obvious and that is- your daughters have men that love them just as much as you love them. Stop acting like a crazy Creole long enough to get to know these young men and thank God for some sons."

He faced her and she stood. "You act like I don't have a right to be mad about how this has gone down! I saved some for you too because you didn't tell me a word!"

"I didn't have to because Merci was only too happy to let you know!"

"Well Nay, at least she gave a doggone enough about me to tell me!"

"Stop acting like a martyr Damas, you know I care!"

He and Nadine stood face-to-face. The foursome on the couch watched the match of wills with awe. Ellen shook her head and wiped tears.

Najid whispered, "Daag, they aint no joke."

Bashan conspired, "Teran gat ih honest."

"Damas ça asé." Mazie's voice and statement of enough stopped her son's diatribe. The room fell silent. Mazie pointed toward a seat, "Nadine asi en lashèj-la." Nadine complied by taking a seat and the act left the foursome open-mouthed. Mazie looked at her son and made the sign for quiet. "Damas fèrmé tô ladjèl."

Nadine mumbled, "Yeah, shut up." The foursome and Ellen snickered until Mazie looked around the room.

"We are family. Make up." The matriarch clapped and waved as if pushing them together.

The women calmed, Najid stood and addressed Damas. "Mr. Buard, we," he pointed between him and Bashan, "would like to talk to you. Is that possible?" Bashan stood next to Najid.

Damas looked at the young men and spoke, "I think it's long overdue." He turned toward Nadine, "Where can we go to make this happen?"

Nadine stood and spoke, "You can stay here and talk. We are going back to Ellen's house to prepare dinner. You have exactly one hour. Damas don't tear up my house. You are not as young as you used to be and these dudes are solid."

Damas laughed, "Woman your mouth should be outlawed in these fifty states. Men talk aint none of your business."

Nadine ushered the women out of the room. As Ellen passed Damas gave her a hug. "We also need to talk, right?" She nodded.

"Nothing changes huh? I get you up in my face and Ellie gets the sweet, we need to talk. Just don't tear up my stuff. Here are the keys, one hour and no more."

"Woman leave! The only time you quiet is when - . Just go so I can talk to these young men Nadine. Have the dinner warm."

Nadine rolled her eyes, "Male chauvinist pig."

Damas laughed, "Barefoot and in the kitchen Nay when I get there you hear me?" She slammed the door and he laughed as he locked it. He came into the living room as the young men gave one another dap.

They all sat and faced each other a minute. "So who are these men that came in and took mô fiy?" He leaned back in his chair commanding their respect.

Bashan spoke up, "Lawd a massi Teran ah har fada's pickney! Straight fi de point lackan arrow an cut lacka razor."

Najid concurred, "Yeah Terry and Nique are definitely their father's daughters. Saadri is more like Miss Ellen and I am happy about that. I can't take all of the mouth." He turned to Damas, "You and Miss Nadine, I don't get it but I do understand Miss Ellen, I don't know Nique's mother."

"They are all a story for another time. You are both men and the Lord will bless you with children one day. If you had daughters that did to you what has happened to me, how would you feel?"

"That's fair Mr. Buard," Najid leaned forward. "I first saw Saadri when she was about sixteen. I had known her before then, she was always good friends with my brother Rasheen. But I saw her when she was sixteen. I didn't approach her until she was coming out of school. I got to know her, I dated her, I pursued her, and I married her over the summer. Prior to meeting you when Saadri was graduating, I honestly thought you were not in the picture. I only saw Miss Ellen and I knew her grandparents were dead. She spoke briefly about your mother Miss Mazie but that was it."

"Siem here, mi tried fi gat Teran fi tell mi bout har fambily but shi wouldn't. Mi used fi gat frustrated trying fi gat har fi open up bout har fambily. Wi almost nuh gat marrid sake ah de way mi found out bout har being Creole an yuh being har fada an nuh de fada of Talib an Ayana, yuh undastan? Wi met deh at school, shi was inna de siem history class. Mi saw har round de school - beautiful an haad fi handle. De fellas couldn't duh nutten wid har quick an biting tongue! Mi watched har an dought bout har until mi couldn't tap tinking bout har. Den a day came wen shi approached mi an afta dat it was ova cah mi knew shi was fi mi. Now wi ah set fi marry inna May."

Damas remained silent. Najid addressed his concern. "I work at the stock exchange sir. Some nights I go to college up in Manhattan. I make a pretty good salary; it's enough for me and Saadri. I plan to save up enough to move us out of here and into a house. Maybe we'll go to Long Island, who knows. The fact is, as long as Saadri is with me we can go wherever. I am sorry things worked out the way they did but I do my best to take care of your daughter. I would like it if we could get to know one another sir?"

Damas looked at Bashan as if to say, your turn. The young men looked at one another before Bashan spoke. "Rite now mi am inna a training program at Grumman. Dey ah sending mi fi school. Wi ave an apartment inna Laurelton, Teran will live dere afta de wedding. Meanwhile wi ah saving an preparing fi wi lives togeda. Mi wud laik fi yuh blessing fi yuh dawta's hand inna marriage."

"I know it's late but I too would like your blessing sir. Saadri and I love one another and we want to know that you accept our love."

Damas sighed, "Mô fiy, like this generation is different and take more chances, more independent. I'm glad you two have it together, I don't have to worry over my daughters so you have my blessings. Now let's get down to business." Damas led them into the kitchen where he prepared drinks.

The young men looked at one another. They thought they were taking care of business.

Chapter 18

Ayana walked into the house and peered into the kitchen, "Ma?" Behind her were Talib and a man who could only have been Butch. Ayana looked at Damas and squinted, "Pe'r Damas?"

"Bonjou Poupé!" He stood and opened his arms for Ayana who flew into them without hesitation.

Talib stood beside his father but said hello as he looked around the kitchen table. He spotted Bashan and yelled, "Shanidoo!" and walked over to him.

"Likkle Mon, wah gwan?" He nodded toward Butch. "Wah gwan?"

Najid nodded toward Butch, "Hey, how you doing?" He then gave dap to Talib.

Butch spoke, "Where's Nadine?"

Damas held onto Ayana, "They over Ellen's fixing dinner, it's time we made our way over. Meet my sons-in-law Najid and Bashan. Najid married Saadri over the summer and Bashan is marrying Teran in the spring. This is Butch y'all, Nadine's estranged husband."

Ayana left Damas' embrace and hugged Najid, "Welcome to the family." She left the kitchen to answer the telephone and took Talib with her.

"Why are y'all here?" Butch scanned the kitchen, bristling at Damas' reference.

Damas sat down at the table but Najid and Bashan remained standing. Najid stared at Butch and their eyes met. Bashan watched a recognition dawn between them and wondered what it was all about. Damas also caught the exchange; he announced, "Butch come on with us over to Ellie's, you know she can cook, you can meet my mother and Nadine is there."

"I'm trying to figure out why she left you here if she is there." Butch remained in place, challenging Damas.

Damas finished his drink. "Family business to take care of; Nay provided me with a space but that's neither here nor there. It's time to eat." He stood from the table. "Fellas, finish those drinks and let's head over to Ellie's."

Ayana appeared in the kitchen, "Pe'r Damas are you leaving because my mother said for me and Talib to come with you, Bashan, and Najid. Daddy, are you coming? Mommy said there is plenty food."

Talib stood in the hall with his coat on, "Come on Daddy, don't leave yet, come with us instead."

Teran answered Ellen's door, "I'm glad you are all here because Mon mon was about to go off on you Pe'r."

Damas entered the apartment first, "Mo lainm twa fiy but your mother makes me want to choke her." He kissed his daughter and took off his coat, then threw over his shoulder, "She's Butch's concern now."

Teran laughed as Ayana entered next and bent to her ear, "You know they had a stand-off in the kitchen." Teran motioned to ask who and Ayana tipped her head toward Butch who walked in behind Talib.

"Hey Dove!" Butch kissed Teran's forehead.

"Hey yourself, you look well. Mommy said you might come and I am glad you're here. Did you meet my fiancé?" Teran smiled and spoke animatedly. She looked around the tall man and spotted Bashan.

Butch turned in the direction of Teran's attention and smiled again. "Bashan and I talked a little on the way over. He seems to have a good head on his shoulders. Good choice."

"Tenk yuh Mista Gregory. Mi cyan wait fah dis beautiful ooman fi be fi mi wife." Bashan walked up to Teran and kissed her mouth. She grinned.

Najid walked in and slapped Bashan on the back, "Control yourself my man! I know you want to throw her over your shoulder and carry her out of here but it's family time." Laughing, he and Bashan high fived one another then he queried, "Where's Candy?"

"She's in the kitchen or in the back. Everyone was busy with something so I got the door." He nodded and walked into the apartment after kissing Teran's cheek.

Teran yelled, "Sè! Tâ ma mari çe li-minn pou twa!" (Sister, your husband is looking for you!) She held Bashan by the hand and led him to an enclave of seats with tray tables set up.

"Yuh affi tell mi wat yuh ah saying," Bashan spoke as he sat. "An wat fi yuh fada said to yuh, mi heard dat before. Yuh said dat to mi."

Teran smiled and kissed him again. "I just called my sister and told her that her husband was looking for her. My father said he loves me but he could choke my mother." They both laughed at the last part.

Bashan stated, "Outta everyone inna dis room mi believe fi yuh fada respects fi yuh mudda de most. Mi kno im loves har but dey could neva ave been marrid." They looked at one another and shook their heads.

"They would have killed one another and I would have been an orphan going between downtown and Cloutierville." The couple laughed before Teran left him to help in the kitchen.

Saadri escorted Najid over to a seat next to Bashan's. He looked up and laughed, "Saadri yuh affi hide de evidence fi yuh lipstick ah smeared." He then looked at Najid and teased, "Wat happened fi control bredda?"

They clasped hands and laughed as Najid sat, "You know these sisters are irresistible, they make a brother lose it."

Bashan snorted, "Yah mon! Dat's wah mek wi ave taken dem off de markit suh quick."

Najid nodded, "Got that right! I been scopin mine a while and caught her at the right time. I can't even entertain the thought of no other dude trying to rap to her. I will nut if somebody try to get with my wife. That girl is my world and I would do anything for her."

"Yuh kno wen wi first met mi nuh tink wi wud gat along but wi ah two sides of de siem coin. Teran ah fi mi world an mi ago kill fah har." Najid held out his hand and Bashan slapped it.

"You good people man. We need to hang out and talk about some things." Najid leaned in. "Let's make that happen soon."
"Yah mon wi will mek ih happen soon." Bashan sensed a turning point in their relationship.

Nadine put the last of the food on a table set up for that purpose. Over her shoulder she spoke, "Did you behave yourself?"

Butch put a hand to his chest. "Me? What makes you think I wouldn't behave myself?"

"Terrence Gregory don't play with me, I know you too well." Nadine sucked her teeth.

He touched a strand of her hair. "You do know me Mrs. Gregory. Of that I have no doubt."

"Butch, were you cool?"

He became exasperated, "Nay aint nobody thinkin about that red nigga! I was cool. Me and him got an understanding. He cock of his walk and I am cock of mine."

Nadine removed his hand, "Boy don't get on my nerves tonight. It's time for us to eat. Sit down and act civilized for once." She brushed by him and called everyone to the meal. He laughed as she walked by. He knew his wife.

Ellen sat Damas in a chair in her room while she sat on the bed. "You're looking good Damas."

Damas lowered his head briefly before speaking, "Ellie, woman I still love you and I will never stop but you have crushed me with this Saadri being married and not telling me. If I could turn back the hands of time things would be different but –"

"You wouldn't have your girls and you know you wouldn't change that. Look I know you're upset but I wasn't trying to hurt you. I have so much going on with my health that I just prayed Saadri and Najid would make it. I am not long for this world and I needed to know she would be alright." Ellen breathed in deeply. "Don't waste time being angry. Enjoy the addition of two young men to the family and support your daughters. They love you and it would crush them if you didn't accept those boys."

Damas nodded, "You are absolutely right Ellie. Marry me so I can take care of you. We have been on hold so long. Marry me and let's ride this out together Ellie."

"Damas I don't have a whole lot of time and I couldn't do that to you. You know I love you and I am sorry I wasted so much time being hurt and trying to hurt you that I didn't do what would have been best for all of us. Now my prayer is for Saadri and Najid and also that God sends you the one you can love and who will love you."

"Ellie I don't care about the time because I have loved and waited for you my whole life. Look, I can come and we can stay here a while until you feel up to coming home with me. I want to take you to the doctor's appointments and take care of you. I can finally relieve some of the strain on Saadri. I know it's been hard on her. Baby, just tell me you'll think about it." Damas was seated beside her on the bed before she realized it.

Ellen saw the grinning young man leaning against a campus tree, "Okay, I'll think about it."

Everyone gathered around the dining table for the blessing of the food. Damas readied himself when Saadri interrupted, "Sitoplé Pe'r, pèrmèt Granmè priyé?"

Mazie stood up and recited the Lord's Prayer.

> "Nouzòt Popá, ki dan syèl-la
>
> Tokin nom, li sinkifyè,
>
> N'ap spéré pou to
>
> rwayomm arivé, é n'a fé ça
>
> t'olé dan syèl ; paréy si la tèr
>
> Donné-nou jordi dipin tou yé jou,
>
> é pardon nouzòt péshé paréy nou pardon
>
> lê moun ki fé nouzòt sikombé tentasyon-la,
>
> Mé délivré nou depi mal."

Afterward she waved her arms over the food and announced, "Astè lésé nou-diné!"

Damas repeated, "She said let us eat, so let us eat!" and started cutting into the roast.

Chapter 19

Much transpired after the early winter showdown. Butch and Nadine reconciled, Ellen consented to marry Damas, Saadri grew concerned over a few late night trips Najid made, Damas forbade Teran from spending the night with Bashan, and Veronique spoke with her sisters about having a boyfriend. For the Christmas holiday the extended family planned a big celebration to be hosted at the home of Teran's grandparents.

At one o'clock Teran, Bashan, Nadine, Butch, Ayana, and Talib walked through the door. Saadri led them into the living room where Ellen stood holding out her hand and Damas stood by grinning.

Nadine announced, "Did you two finally do it? Is that a wedding ring?"

Ellen nodded with tears down her face, "Yes Nay, we got married."

"Well about time! Congratulations Mr. and Mrs. Buard!" Nadine grabbed them both in a hug that lasted several seconds before the group realized she was talking to them.

Saadri led the rest into the kitchen where Teran began questions. "Sè how does it feel to have your parents married? When did they do this? Where's Najid? Don't they look happy? Where's Pe'r going to live? Here? Are they moving to Texas?"

Bashan probed, "Fi yuh fada lives inna Texas?"

Butch also asked, "So many questions Teran? Which do you want her answer first?"

Saadri laughed, "Oh, I am doing it again. I probably would be a great interrogator."

Teran laughed and was about to speak when they heard Damas, "Aou zòt mô fiy?" (Where are my children?)

The sisters answered, "En lakizinn–la Pe'r" (In the kitchen daddy)

Damas walked into the kitchen and hugged Teran, "You still love me Shaer?"

Teran kissed her father's cheek, "Of course Pe'r. You and Mon mon never would have worked. Mon mon Ellen is more to your liking."

Butch laughed, "Me and Nadine barely work!"

Nadine yelled, "And we won't if you keep putting your foot in your mouth!"

Bashan laughed aloud and Butch turned to him. "Don't be too entertained, you are marrying her daughter. The fruit doesn't fall far from the tree."

Bashan countered, "Teran an mi ave an undastandin, rite babi, cah shi kno mi nuh romp dat!"

Teran swatted Bashan's arm and Damas spoke, "That's it Son, you have to know how to handle them. That one in there," he nodded in Nadine's direction, "is pure fire and will scorch you! Butch you have my sympathy."

Butch laughed and the women appeared in the kitchen. Nadine tilted her head toward Butch who held up his arms in surrender. "That was Damas!"

She looked at Damas who still embraced Teran and said, "Merry Christmas to you too! Let me get a picture of this moment, you two stay right there." After she snapped a picture she had everyone strike different poses. The kitchen exploded with laughter when Ayana got

Nadine and Damas to pose nicely for a picture. The last photo they captured was Damas holding Ellen around the waist. Their smiles spoke of their sublime happiness.

Teran stood next to Saadri, "Aou çé tâ mari?"

Saadri sighed and pulled Teran into her room, "I don't know where he is Sè. Lately he has been more elusive and I can't ask him about what's going on without him getting upset and telling me not to question him like he's a child. So I keep quiet and focus on my mother and try to figure out what the heck to do with my life. I don't want Pe'r asking any questions but he'll be around more. I just don't know Teran."

"What's the matter Candy?" Najid hugged Teran and took Saadri in his arms. "It's Christmas so everything else can wait, right?" He stared at her a moment and Saadri nodded affirmatively. He then descended on Saadri's lips in a kiss that winded Teran, the man was raw virility.

Awed by proof of what Veronique told her about Najid being able to communicate without speaking, Teran blinked. "Bon Krismis Najid." He grinned and wrapped an arm around each sister.

Damas stepped into the doorway. "We head downtown in twenty minutes piti." He turned but not before he looked from Saadri to Najid to make sure all was well. Teran followed her father out of the room to distract him and join the rest of the family.

Three carloads traveled thirty minutes to the Jackson's downtown home in Clinton Hill, Brooklyn. In the Monte Carlo the couples listened to WBLS play Christmas songs by artists like the Whispers and the Temptations. The foursome sang along as they coasted down Atlantic Avenue. Najid held Saadri close, kissed her several times and spoke, "Yo B, man, we have to chill more often. We was maxin and I enjoyed that man."

"Anytime mon, wi cya chill anytime." Bashan looked at Najid through the rearview mirror.

Teran looked back at her sister, "Did you know they went out together?" Saadri shook her head.

"Teran wat de problem? Yuh tink wi affi tell yuh wen wi ah going out?"

Najid blew out a breath, "You buggin! Our names aint Butch!"

"Najid that wasn't nice!" Saadri hit his arm and he threw her a look to say she'd better not do it again. She emphasized, "That was uncalled for."

Teran was irritated by Najid's treatment of her sister and his attitude. "I am not buggin and I didn't say anyone had to tell me. I was surprised that you two had gone out so don't get all cave man on me. And what do you have against Butch? The temperature goes down twenty degrees when you two get around one another."

Najid cocked his head, "I seen dude around and he aint squeaky clean but I'm a parlay in the cut cause he's your mom's husband."

Teran turned her body toward him, "Don't play me to the left either. What do you know?"

Saadri sat up from their embrace and looked at him. Najid looked between them. "You see this B? They double teaming me with this twin thing back here. It's buggin me out 'cause they look so much alike."

Stopped at a light, Bashan watched the scene and laughed, "Nuh dem perfected dat double team? Yuh cyan get outta dat trap." He continued to drive.

"Okay, so I know dude uses and I just hope your moms won't have any grief because of it." Najid held his hands forward as if to say that's it.

Teran turned back around, "It makes sense why he had to leave the last time."

Saadri touched her shoulder, "Mo shagrin Sè."

Teran grabbed her sister's hand. "It's okay Sè. For all my mother's kick butt attitude about life it seems it hasn't worked for her always. She ends up with this additional set of headaches. Well, I can't do anything about this but I can marry my baby and live my life in better circumstances."

"Yuh gat dat rite! Mi am moving yuh into a ouse pon tim ahland as soon as mi can. Yuh will gimmi sum pickney an mi am coming home fi yuh everi night."

Najid reached up and clapped Bashan's shoulder. "That's what I'm talkin about boy! Get these women hooked up in a nice crib somewhere and make love to them without everybody hearing and make a house full of kids. Bring that check home, have a hot meal cooked – that's the life. Shoot we can be neighbors, you let me know where you going on the Island. You want to go on the Island Candy?"

Saadri laughed, "Oh you top billing today! We going on the Island now? Sure, you take me there I will go." She and Teran laughed.

"Wi may nuh waan dem dat close fi one anoda. Dem wi be able fi double team wi everi day." Bashan feigned a grimace as he spoke.

Najid leaned up to Bashan's seat, "But yo check it, we know how to slam dunk on them. They know who wears the pants and puts the lights out."

The sisters squealed. Teran spoke first, "You so fresh Najid! And don't be agreeing with him Shan!"

Bashan spoke "Nuh affi cah yuh kno mi romp haad."

"Oh Lord! Y'all romp in the romper room!" Saadri commented as she and Najid burst into laughter.

Teran turned toward her sister, "Yeah and you get your lights put out! I'm telling Pe'r!"

Saadri laughed enough to have tears in her eyes. "You brat." She couldn't stop laughing. After a moment Teran joined in too.

Chapter 20

Bashan got them to the Clinton Hill home in a fit of laughter. The other carload met them at the door.

Damas saw the foursome and asked, "What's going on?"

Najid answered, "Folks just rompin lights out that's all." They snickered but then broke into laughter after watching Damas' expression of confusion.

Ellen touched her husband's arm. "Leave them baby. It's young people talk. I don't always understand them either."

The smell of good home cooking and Mrs. Jackson met them as they walked through the door. The silver-haired, brown woman kissed and hugged everyone. Mr. Jackson called from a back room where the men of the family assembled. The group walked to the room and greeted everyone. Mr. Jackson saw Damas and stood from his chair, "Damas you aint dead yet? I aint see you in a month of Sundays boy!" Damas laughed and grabbed Mr. Jackson in a bear hug. "It's good to see you too Gordon. I brought my wife with me."

Gordon Jackson looked around and said, "Where is she?" Damas pointed to Ellen and Mr. Jackson was shocked, "After all these years you finally wore Ellie down! Come here and give me some sugar my little Chocolate Drop!" He gingerly kissed the obviously frail Ellen.

"How are you Mr. G?" Ellen laid a manicured hand on Mr. Jackson's chest. "You are looking well. It's good to see you."

Gordon replied, "It's always good to see you Ellie." He looked at Damas and said, "You make sure you take care of my Chocolate Drop because she needs tender love and care. She's a lady you know." He smiled and released Ellen to Damas. "Speaking of which, where is my Amazon child? Nadine your daddy don't get a Merry Christmas?!" Nadine yelled greetings from the kitchen.

Teran laughed and stepped in front of her grandfather with Bashan, "Merry Christmas Granddaddy. I brought Bashan with me."

Bashan joked, "Shi brought mi but mi drove de cyar. Merry Christmas Mr. Jackson!" They slapped one another's shoulders.

Saadri came next, "Merry Christmas Granddaddy. This is my husband Najid."

"Husband! When did all of this happen?" Mr. Jackson looked completely shocked.

Damas answered with, "Imagine how I felt when I found out. They went to the justice of the peace summer before last."

Gordon Jackson shook his head, "You don't say. Well welcome to the family-"

Saadri answered with, "Najid, Granddaddy."

"Najid, welcome. So are you an Indian? You are named like the musician." Gordon grasped his hand and pumped vigorously.

Najid grinned, "Hello Sir, my family is from Texas and the musician is Najee."

Gordon joked, "The U.N. don't have a thing on my family: Creole, Jamaican, and now Texas."

Saadri frowned, "Granddaddy Texas is not another country it's part of the United States."

"No ma'am Texas is its own country!" Gordon broke into a peal of laughter.

Najid agreed, "You have a point there."

Gordon sat back in his recliner as Ayana and Talib came in to greet him briefly. He became comfortable and declared, "Damas go on over there to the bar and fix us up. Fellas," he nodded to Bashan and Najid, "take a load off. Let me show you what good music sounds like. Terry, you and Dri go and please get that wife of mine to speed it up. Look, try to bring me a sandwich or something to keep me from starving back here." The sisters exited with Ellen laughing as Butch entered the room and they heard Gordon wish him a Merry Christmas.

At six Najid and Saadri left with Teran and Bashan so they could spend time with Najid's parents. Mrs. Jackson sent the couples along with food and desert. Teran and Saadri got into the back seat together.

"You see this B. They kicked me out of the back seat. I wanted to snuggle with my baby." Najid closed the door after he made sure the young women were in securely.

Bashan turned to the sisters and said, "Dis double team bizniz mus tap."

Teran rejoined, "You have been with the men all afternoon so stay with your boy up there and leave us to our girl talk."

Najid and Bashan looked at one another and laughed. "Oh man they are jealous so they are giving us the cold shoulder." Najid rubbed a gloved hand over his face and leaned his head back against the seat.

"Dats okay taak now an wi romp lata." He started the car.

Najid rolled with laughter, "You a wild boy B! Candy you know what time it is!"

The ladies sucked their teeth as the fellas laughed in the front seat. It put Bashan in a good mood. "Teran duh yuh waan fi tap an see Fawn an Reggie fi a short while?"

Saadri answered, "That would be nice; we haven't seen them since the wedding. She must be ready to pop any day now."

Najid shook his head, "And you answer for one another too. Y'all should have been twins and made life easier on everyone. How do you assume we are invited Mrs. Raenier?"

Saadri leaned toward her husband, "Since you have to know everything Mr. Raenier they live in Crown Heights which is on our way home. It makes no sense to pass their house to drop us off to double back and then go out to Queens." She and Teran gave each other a high five.

Najid turned around and looked at his wife. He smiled, "When the lights are out I am going to make you eat those words."

Saadri inhaled, "You aren't playing fair."

Najid winked at her, "I play for keeps."

Reggie answered the door in good spirits. "Cha! Mi bredren, sistren dem!" He spied Bashan and held his hand out for a dap. "Wa'ppun mi key?" They greeted one another before Reggie called again, "Fawn cum yah!"

Fawn wobbled toward the door to greet them. "Teran! Saadri! Shan! Saadri's husband!"

Everyone laughed as Najid bent to kiss Fawn, "Hi Fawn, it's Najid."

Fawn held onto his arm, "I am so sorry but since I have been pregnant it seems like my brain cells have gone on vacation."

Teran hugged her, "No that's not the reason. I told you to stop hanging out with the young and the foolish." She nodded toward Reggie and Fawn giggled while he grabbed Teran in a bear hug.

"Wi will ave none of dat! Merry Christmas Teran."

Saadri wrapped her arm in Fawn's as they walked into the house, "You look so pretty girl. It's good to see you."

Fawn gushed, "Thanks Dri! You look good yourself, marriage agrees with you."

"I do what I can." They laughed as Najid followed behind the two ladies.

Everyone settled into the living room and Reggie became the ultimate host. "Cya mi get mi breddas sup'm fi drink? De gyal dem waan a drink?"

Bashan stretched his long legs as he positioned himself comfortably in an oversized armchair. "Yuh ave Red Stripe Reg? Mi could use a cold one."

Teran sat on his lap, "Shan, you had a few drinks at my grandparents', that's why we left so late. I wanted to make sure you were good to drive."

Bashan looked from Teran to Reggie, "Mi empress nuh waan mi fi drink suh mi ave a cola. Dis a gud day mi nuh waan spile it."

Najid relaxed on the loveseat and gently pulled Saadri to sit next to him. "I could use a beer though, I aint driving." Saadri looked at him but said nothing. Najid watched her and returned an exasperated look at Reggie. "Never mind man, bring me some soda or something. The Mrs. don't want me to drink anymore either."

"I didn't say anything Najid." Saadri grinned. The room laughed.

"Yuh usband kno yuh Twin suh don't behave as eff im nuh kno wat blowing out yuh breat' mean!" Everyone laughed again as Reggie left the living room to retrieve refreshments.

Teran couldn't believe how big Fawn had gotten. "Girl when are you going in? You like you are about to bust!"

"Sè! That was rude. She knows she is growing, she has to live with it." Najid looked at his wife with pride.

Fawn replied. "It's good having you around Saadri because you know Teran never knows what to say. You're right, I'll be glad when this is over. We are counting the days because I am due and could go in at any time."

"Yuh look beautiful Fawn. Yuh wi be a gud mudda. Mi an Teran ah happy fah yuh an Reg." He cradled Teran's body as he spoke.

"Thanks Bashan, so what is everyone up to?" Reggie came back with drinks and snacks as Fawn stretched out on the couch.

Teran excitedly caught her up on the last few months. "We really have lost touch, so much has happened. Pe'r came to town early last month and he was pissed!"

Saadri added, "He had us quaking in our skin but we were to blame because we didn't tell him about Najid and Bashan."

Fawn yelled, "What?! Oh I know Pe'r Damas went ape on your behinds! I missed it, shoot! Oooh did he and Miss Nadine-"

Najid cut in, "Head-to-head! That was a treat. Miss Nadine is no joke and she will take Mr. B on in a heartbeat!" Bashan burst into laughter and dapped Najid again. The sisters looked at them as if they were foreign beings.

Teran elbowed his rib cage but Bashan went on undisturbed, "Likkle Momma Nay inna Mista Buard face and im vex but shi nuh care. Mi dought dem wud box!"

"Wa'ppen? Dem box inna de ouse? Teran likkle mudda box har daddy? Mi cyan imagine dat scene." Reggie shook his head and chuckled.

"Oh it was a real treat Reg!" Najid sat forward. "I have big respect for Miss Nadine though. She was defending her girls and Mr. B really couldn't come back at her on the points she was making. Then he turned on me and B but we handled ours too! We knew our turn was coming--"

Reggie asked, "Yuh large up yuself, ee?" He made a motion of standing taller so Najid could better catch his meaning.

"Yeah man, you know we did. Bottom line is they are our women now and Pops or no Pops we weren't going to let him go but so far. They were petrified, he broke them down to tears, and you know a man won't stand by and let his woman get bullied by nobody so we had to respectfully let Pops know we got this." He made a hand motion between him and Saadri and repeated it for Bashan and Teran.

Reggie sat back on the couch and placed Fawn's legs in his lap. "Yah mon. De gyal dem nuh undastan ou haad fi be a mon cyan be, whole heap de respons."

Bashan nodded his head as he joined in, "Mi told Teran dat very ting. Reg, Santa did bring yuh wat yuh waan?"

Reggie brightened and removed his wife's legs to her dismay. "Bredren cum yah, wi ago inna de basement. Mi show yuh ting an ting." The men left the room without a word to the women.

Teran continued. "So, we have our apartment in Laurelton, I got a raise on the job, I am thinking about taking the civil service test, school is going well, we set the wedding for May, our families are helping a lot with the festivities and have given us many things for the apartment and we are saving money."

Fawn nodded her head and smiled. "You two have been productive, that's good. I'm glad things are going so well. So May it is, I hope I can lose enough weight to look decent in my dress. I am standing with two supermodels and I don't want to look like the homely housewife."

Saadri laughed, "Stop it girl. We are not supermodels and you could never look like a homely anything. When is the baby due?"

"The doctors said the middle of January. I hope it is on time because I have to get my body back together." Fawn looked at them and lowered her voice. "I am glad they are gone because I have something to tell you." The sisters leaned forward as she continued, "We have a situation on our hands. This co-worker of Reggie's named Andrea-"

"That was the skeezer at the wedding Sè, remember, the one Bashan drove home?"

Saadri affirmed, "Yes I remember. We had to keep Veronique from clocking her. Maybe we should have let her loose."

A frown appeared on Fawn's face, "What in the world happened, at my wedding?" The sisters nodded as she continued, "Well it seems the skeezer strikes again because she bought my husband a g-string for Christmas and from what Reggie told me she bought some for all of the men on the job." With that Fawn raised her eyebrow.

Two pairs of eyes looked in Teran's direction; she could feel a headache mounting. "How many times must I hear this skeezer's name?"

Saadri stared wide-eyed, "Well how many times have you heard it and why haven't you told me?"

Teran knew her sister would feel hurt if she thought she was deliberately left out. "Dri you have had so much to deal with and Bashan and I have been weathering storms and riding waves. I didn't say anything because we are trying to keep things within our relationship, you know, not bringing everyone into what we alone should be dealing with. But we had a pretty big fight over this chick. One of his so-called friends dimed him out that they were meeting her and some of her friends up at Bentleys. I went off but Shan maintained that he was going up there to introduce her and that so-called friend, who by the way was trying to make a play for me. Shan's friends had to get the guy out of the apartment before Shan destroyed him. Then we started fighting and his father and stepmother had to break us up."

"He put his hands on you Terry?!" Saadri stood up. "I will shoot him myself!"

Teran jumped to her sister's side wide-eyed with alarm. "Dri no, no! He didn't hit me. I actually hit him, quite a few times. He grabbed me to shake me and stop me from fighting him but I went ballistic."

"Just like Miss Nadine and Pe'r Damas, a chip off the old block." Fawn shook her head and reclined on the couch. "Teran what can you do with that mountain of a man but get shook? You my girl and got much heart but you are a trip. I guess you would have to be just like your parents because neither of them is scared of much including each other!" Fawn started laughing.

Saadri watched Fawn a moment. "I guess you have a point there." She too found amusement.

Teran sat in the chair she vacated. "Later for both of you, back to this skeezer, Shan didn't say anything to me about any drawers and we've been together all day." She closed her eyes and breathed a few deep breaths.

Saadri walked over and gathered Teran to her midsection. Teran wrapped her arms around her older sister. Fawn spoke as the consolation continued. "I guess there is no other way to find out than to ask. I went off this morning when Reggie showed them to me."

The men walked into the living room as the scene unfolded and Najid voiced for them. "I guess we all know about the freaky-deaky Christmas gift. From where I stand this is obviously a case of homegirl not understanding her place. I say the fellas need to make her know where she stands with them once and for all. Personally, I would not wear dental floss and would not appreciate the gift."

A peal of hoots emitted from all as the last statement replayed in their minds. Bashan looked at Teran's tears and walked over to where she sat. He bent in front of her and looked at Saadri who moved to give them a moment. "Babi yuh believe mi nuh liad wen mi seh mi nuh kno bout de present? Wi been togedda aal di while todeh an aal mi presents at de ouse fa wi fi open lata. Teran mi nuh waan nuh present laik dat fram anoda ooman. Andrea nuh easy."

She looked at her fiancé and smiled in spite of her throbbing heart. "I just keep hearing her name Shan and I am finished with it. Set her straight like Najid said, once and for all."

"Yes, you set her straight or I will come up to Grumman and wait for her and if she doesn't say what I want to hear I will knock the taste buds out of her mouth." Saadri loomed.

"Whoa Candy! Baby what's the matter with you? You all over B like you are trying to run up on him. He didn't know that freak was going to do this. They work with her so let them handle it the right way. Who are you supposed to be – Kung Fu Mama?" Najid moved her to the side so they could talk in private.

Teran snickered, "He is full of jokes tonight isn't he?" Fawn hid her laughter as well.

"Teran mi nuh liad. Andrea did rude an mi vex. Truss mi babi mi tek care fi dat. Aal mi waan ih yuh inna mi ouse an mi life." Bashan grabbed Teran into his arms and approached her lips. She did not disappoint him.

Najid whispered into Saadri's ear, "See what I told you?" He nudged her forward.

"Ahem." Bashan looked up from the elongated kiss he shared with his fiancé into Saadri's identical face. "I am sorry for going off on you."

Bashan stood and embraced her, "Yuh ah mi sista suh mi cyan get bringly wit yuh. Yuh duh luv Teran." He then looked at Teran and declared, "Babi, mi luv yuh cyan done."

Najid walked up behind Saadri and wrapped his arms around her waist. "See baby, your sister got that boy's heart."

Teran answered, "He has mine too."

Chapter 21

Damas moving into the apartment caused a greater strain on Najid and Saadri as they were constantly under his scrutiny and subject to his comments regarding the health and progress of their marriage. Najid's absence on some nights caused Damas to question his activities and Saadri found her excuses running out. Ellen did what she could to keep her husband occupied but within the confines of the small apartment it was not easy to maintain privacy or boundaries. The women prayed earnestly for their men and maintained faith that God would provide the respite they sought. When Veronique called and invited her sisters to Greek Weekend, it was a welcomed reprieve from the household tension.

"Roxanne, Roxanne" by UTFO blared through the gym as the crowd cheered and danced. The guest emcee, a popular mix master, announced, "Alright, alright! Let's give it up for the lovely ladies of Lambda Theta Chi Sorority – Incorporated!!!!!!"

Saadri turned to Teran, "This is Sè's group, right?"

Teran wrinkled her nose, "I think so." They stood along with the rest of the college students packed into the gym of Forsica University where Veronique attended. The cheers were deafening but the young women were having a wonderful time.

"Çé lá Dell, li zami mé, aou çé nô Sè?" (There is Dell, I see her there, where is our sister?) Saadri spotted Veronique's best friend Dell but could not locate her sister. Teran shrugged until they spotted Veronique in another line from Dell's. The group of ladies danced into the gym as if they owned it. They cheered. "Kabalé Sè, kabalé," for their older sister.

Just behind them a young man gave a wolf call and others joined in. Teran turned and looked into the handsome face of Bobby Lattimore, Veronique's boyfriend. Beside him was Dell's boyfriend Maurice "Eddie" Eddrington who was a basketball star at the school. The men looked at her and smiled. Teran turned back to the performance as the ladies stepped with precision creating their own version of the song they entered on. "Lambda, Lambda! We know we own these streets. Lambda, Lambda! No others can compete!"

Saadri clapped and cheered as Eddie commented loud enough for Bobby and the ladies to hear. "I could kiss they Daddy for making these fine thangs! They all fine! What y'all say a few minutes ago?"

Saadri answered, "Kabalé, party or dance, celebrate. We told our sister to party hearty." She deliberately addressed the answer to Bobby.

Eddie touched Teran's hair and she shot him a warning look. "Y'all all have that pretty color and pretty hair too. You didn't get this red out of nobody's bottle."

Teran shook her head as she watched the group's performance. "No, this is all me."

He would have said more but the crowd responded when the ladies sent a barb to a rival sorority. Bobby let out another wolf call and the others followed. Teran looked at Saadri and they giggled before she whispered, "Didn't you tell me to watch out for wolves in sheep's clothing."

Saadri leaned into her and said, "I know, right." They giggled again. "Veronique, bon louvraj!" She shouted as the sorors finished the last step.

Teran shouted, "Laissez les bon temps rouler!" Many in the nearby audience turned to look at Teran who in turn waved and sat down. Laughter ensued in her section. The group left and as they ended the show, the audience socialized while awaiting the judges' decision.

Eddie leaned forward, "What that mean sexy lady?"

Teran turned to him, "Let the good times roll and my name is Teran."

Eddie laughed, "Good times indeed Teran. And I beg to differ on that sexy note. Lawd y'all some fine sisters. Who's the oldest?"

Saadri answered, "Veronique."

Eddie rejoined, "No I mean between you and your twin. Who came first?"

They both said, "We're not twins."

Bobby laughed, "Eddie they aren't, Roni told me they look and act like twins but they are not. When I saw them I bugged out too because they are just about identical."

Eddie looked at both of them, "You don't know which one to pick they both so fine."

Teran answered, "The answer is choose door number three because we aren't an option. Besides you have Dell, my sister," she nodded her head toward Saadri, "is married and I have a fiancé."

Bobby laughed and Eddie coughed, "Married and engaged! I commend those brothers for getting you off the yard but I am also mad I didn't get a chance."

Teran responded with, "You never had one."

Bobby and Saadri burst into laughter and Eddie looked at her, "Wow Miss New York! Are y'all all this blunt?"

"Yes." Teran turned to Saadri who was still laughing.

Saadri looked at Teran and shook her head, "Nadine Jr."

The weekend progressed with its share of drama and Saadri could tell Veronique wasn't as happy as she let on. She was unsure Bobby and Veronique would make it as a couple although she felt Bobby was a great guy. Sunday morning brought a storm of censure once Najid and Bashan entered Veronique's apartment. They came down to bring Saadri and Teran home. Their surprisingly open hostility toward Bobby caused angst and Saadri sensed the timing was right to speak to the group about accepting Christ in their lives, which they did. Najid was peaceful on the ride home and she prayed the change would impact his street activities.

May 1985

Najid walked into the bedroom near nine o'clock on a Saturday night and Saadri could smell alcohol on his breath. She moved away and finished putting clothes into a dresser drawer. He moved to her side and wrapped his arms around her waist. After planting a kiss on her neck he announced, "Let's make a baby Candy."

Saadri massaged her temple. He had to be joking. "Najid, we don't even have a place of our own. I am not about to bring a baby in here. It's already cramped."

Najid threw his hat on the windowsill. "Hmm, well I just recently won the privilege of being openly acknowledged as your husband but I guess I am getting ahead of myself to think we should really make this a marriage and start a family."

She turned to look at him and saw in his stare a readiness to lash out. She braced herself. "Baby —"

"Oh so I am your baby now? But you just won't have my baby. We are here because your mother has been sick and I know you want to be near her. I would like for her to see a grandchild before she leaves us you know."

Her eyes teared and she moved to get away from him but he wouldn't let her move. "Stop it! I can't do this with you."

Najid snarled into her ear, "Do what? I'm talking to you."

Saadri challenged, "No you're not, you're being mean and I am not going to let you mistreat me." She tried to move again and he pushed her down on the bed. Saadri gasped.

"Since when is a man talking to his wife and asking for a baby being mean? I bust my butt day in and day out for you girl."

"Najid you are out there in those streets doing what you do and that has nothing to do with me. You didn't even have the courtesy to come to my sister's wedding. Mon mon couldn't be there because she was still in the hospital but you should have been there."

He nodded, "See, that's the real problem. You're mad because I couldn't go to Teran's wedding. Bashan is my man so if I couldn't make it you should know it had to be a legitimate reason."

Saadri rolled to the other side of the bed and replied, "The streets is not a legitimate reason. That was a special family event and I am there without you. How do you think it made me feel?"

Najid rounded the bed and grabbed Saadri about the waist, "I know you don't like some of what I have to do but trust me; it's for you ultimately. There's not a day I don't pray for things to be different Candy."

She cried, "Let me help you."

"Just love me Candy, I need your love and support." He sat on the bed and brought her to his lap.

The early June afternoon was pleasant as Saadri stepped onto the Baldwin Station platform to spend time with her sister and brother-in-law and see the new Long Island home Bashan's parents gifted to them. Teran was waiting as she said and Saadri thought to herself Bashan was having a positive impact on her perpetually late sister. "Hello Mrs. Watts, it's good to see you. Are you pregnant yet?"

Teran gasped, "Ki t'alé fé to-mèmm Sè?"

Saadri placed a hand on her hip, "I look like the hell I am going through, I haven't done anything to myself, to answer your question." She hugged Teran. "You are looking good, marriage agrees with you." They walked arm–in–arm out of the lobby. "Aou çé mâ bofrèr?"

"Shan is at the house." Teran hid a smirk.

Saadri frowned, "Are we taking a cab?"

"No." Teran kept walking.

Saadri stopped her, "How are we getting there? Can we walk?"

"We are a fifteen minute car ride away so we are not walking. Cum ya, I'm over here." Teran walked toward the car and felt alone so she turned to find Saadri staring wide–eyed at her. "What's wrong Sè? Leggo!"

Saadri burst into laughter, "You have been around Shan and his family so long that you don't even realize how you are starting to use some of their sayings, 'cum ya, leggo'! Girl you are too much, wait - !"

"What now?" Teran looked at her sister in mock frustration.

Saadri placed a hand over her mouth before declaring, "You are driving now."

Teran laughed, "Yep, I was wondering when you would pick up on that. I officially got my license just before the wedding. Shan had been teaching me for a while. He got tired of chauffeuring me around as he put it. So yes, I drive now."

"Congratulations, the baby is truly growing up." Saadri opened the passenger door and got in the car.

Teran looked at her, "Do you want anything? I made a cake, some lunch and some red zinger iced tea. I even picked up some movies from the video store."

"No, that sounds delicious. I don't need anything else." Saadri laid her head back.

At the house everyone had lunch before Bashan went into the living room to watch a movie. The sisters sat in the kitchen's banquette.

"You are going to talk to me Saadri Raenier. You look absolutely worn out." Teran touched her hand.

"Mon mon is in her last days Teran."

"No Saadri! I thought she could get a transplant and get better."

"Sè the cancer came back and spread so there won't be any transplants." Saadri sighed heavily.

"How is Pe'r taking this?"

"About as good as can be expected. She is the love of his life and he had so little time with her as his wife."

Teran shook her head, "What do you want to do? What do you need from me?"

"This is enough, you are married now and that is a lot of responsibility. Just being here for me like this is more than enough." Saadri moved to sit on the same side of the banquette as Teran. They leaned their heads together and spoke softly. "I have gone through so many emotions and I know these are the stages of grief. Now I just want her to stop suffering and if that has to happen only through her death then I know we'll see each other again on the other side."

Teran cried, "You two have always been so different, so at peace."

Saadri squeezed Teran's hand. "But you have that peace now because you accepted Christ."

"I know Dri but not like you. I am happy but I think something may be missing."

"Like what? You have a husband who adores you, a supportive family, and your health, not to mention this big beautiful house you two are going to fill up with babies. I'm surprised you're not pregnant already." Saadri nudged her.

"We just got married a month ago. Give me some time to adjust to my new life." Teran thought a moment, "Where's Najid?"

"He's back in those streets and I am so hurt. His family is worried and even his mother is not supporting his behavior. With Mon mon being sick I haven't really had the time to focus on him. I think that too is driving a wedge between us. I am spending so much time with Mon mon and Pe'r that Najid is secondary and that is not good medicine for a strong marriage. Remember that Teran. Don't make Bashan second to anyone or anything or you'll pay for it like I am. Just keep us in your prayers Sè." Saadri cried softly as Teran wiped her tears with her shirt.

"Saadri yeye wata?" Bashan sat across from them and watched them with a smile. "Yuh mus ave luk laik dis wen yuh were likkle gyal dem. Suh innocent an laik twins. Wah gwan? Najid ah inna truble?"

Saadri nodded as she let go of the pain she apparently held at bay. Teran spoke, "Baby, Mon Mon Ellie is dying and Najid went back out into the streets. He and Saadri are having a hard time of it right now."

"Ou yuh fada?" Bashan got up to retrieve tissue. He gave it to Saadri and went to the stove.

Teran held and rocked her sister while Bashan answered the ringing phone and attended to what he had on the stove. He finished within ten minutes and returned to the banquette.

"Saadri tek de cup. Dis will mek yuh sleep betta. Yuh need fi rest an dis will help." He placed a cup of tea in front of her.

Teran remarked, "Ooh Shan made his toddy for you. You are going to love it and it will help you sleep for sure. Drink all of it."

Saadri took a sip, "Umm this is good; did you put cinnamon in it?"

Bashan snorted, "Mi put a few different tings inna ih. Drink up."

Teran rubbed Saadri's back as she drained the cup. "Come Dri let's take you upstairs and let you rest a while."

Saadri nodded as she walked out of the kitchen with Teran, "Shan may I have another cup? That was really good."

Bashan stood with his hands behind his back looking satisfied. "Sure mi ago bring ih rite wey."

The next afternoon Teran and Bashan brought Saadri home and visited with Ellen in her weakened condition. Najid's absence was palpable, Damas and Bashan talked at length about many things including Najid and Saadri. Bashan found himself promising Damas he would talk to the young man to quell the tension.

Chapter 22

Najid held Saadri's hand during the funeral. He was concerned. She ran around making sure everything was the way her mother would have wanted it and barely slept. His mother warned him of Saadri's impending collapse. All of their close friends, who were there to support the couple, also warned him of Saadri overcompensating. He gave her a sidelong glance and could see Saadri was not focused on anything in particular. Najid tried to pull her closer but she was stiff. He slid closer, leaned into her body, and wondered if Saadri truly registered his presence. His heart ached for her and for the fact that he was powerless to change the circumstances.

On the other side of him sat Damas, equally stiff, aged at least ten years. Najid made a fist and gave him a light 'dap'. Damas looked at him and Najid could see the equal parts of disappointment and comfort the older man struggled with. He couldn't blame Damas for the position he was now in. Najid prayed for a resolution because he did not want to lose his wife, his family, his life.

The Pastor of the church, Kent Sailor, delivered a powerful sermon about the measure of a woman's life and Najid found many points stirred a chord within him. When the pastor gave the altar call Najid seriously contemplated stepping forward but knew he had to when he saw Bashan and Teran moving out of their seats. He looked around the packed sanctuary and could see many who were moved by the call; he knew Ellen Buard must be smiling from heaven. One set of eyes disturbed him though, those of Mary Clark; Najid blinked to be sure he read the emotion in those eyes correctly, they read of hatred. He'd been in the streets long enough to know there was a devil that never wanted men to get ahead. In Mary's eyes he saw that devil but he refused to allow her or that force to stop him from making a sincere change, no matter the consequences. He got up, grabbed Teran's hand to let her know she and Bashan had company. As they continued to move toward the altar he felt someone grab his free hand – Veronique.

The pastor was overjoyed as he watched the immediate family then friends step forward and that the Spirit had granted Ellen's final wish. He spoke under his breath, "Evangelist Ellie you done good."

Saadri was stunned by the altar response and overwhelmed to see her family become the first partakers. She cried over the goodness of God to allow her mother's passing to be the gate to their salvation and recommitment. She cried over her sisters' and brother-in-law's rededication. She cried over the acceptance of her Mon mon Nadine, Butch and her father – no one could get them into a church let alone to the altar. Most of all she cried for her husband who she knew was battling demons. She asked God to protect him from himself and others and thanked Him for drawing Najid closer.

Many well-wishers filed past Saadri and she looked at them without truly seeing them; she nodded her head yet uttered not one word. There was no more to be said because her mother was gone and she could do no more about that. Then her father stepped in front of her, Saadri looked into Damas Buard's soft hazel eyes and saw why her mother fell for the handsome man. He must have been heavenly twenty years earlier, before her birth, for he was quite handsome still. Saadri opened her mouth, "Mo lainm twa Pe'r." (I love you daddy) Damas nodded and pulled her into an embrace.

Najid held an emotional Veronique as he watched Saadri and Damas. He saw the family more clearly than he'd ever seen them; they were broken just as he was broken and through all the brokenness Ellen loved them and led them to Christ. He shook his head and Veronique jibed, "I know the Hard Rock is not crying!"

He looked at her mascara-blackened eyes and quipped, "Elvira is talking?" She nudged him and they walked back to the seats where the family prepared for the recessional. They marched out and were met by a throng of people who managed to separate them from the rest of the family.

Najid and Veronique found Saadri surrounded by a swarm of matrons. Much to his chagrin, Mary Clark held center court. He walked up to the group calmly. The women stopped fussing over Saadri and fixed Najid with steely gazes. Instantly he knew his reputation among the women was unfavorable. Mary barely looked at him, "She'll be fine. She's just upset over everybody in her face. No one is over here watching this child."

Najid purposely stalled. He would have set them to running for safety had he not stopped to consider his actions. "Saadri, it's time we headed to the cemetery baby. Let's go."

Mary stood and squared off with Najid. "Stop trying to order her around like she's your child or something!"

Najid stepped a little closer to Mary, "What goes on between me and my wife is none of your business. Remember that."

Mary was incensed, "Who do you think you are? You don't scare me with your thuggish self! Someone should have whipped your behind a long time ago, then you may have become a decent man!"

Veronique sprang into action, "A mean old biddy, that's what you are! Mind your business! He's talking to his wife!"

Several of the women in the group pulled Mary away from Najid and Veronique. One of them, a short stout woman of dark complexion spoke to Najid. "You held your peace while she had her say and I like that. You have respect and you are right, some things folk ought not get into. Take that child out of here so she can put her mama away. We can handle Mary." She looked at Veronique with censure but moved Mary away.

When the women moved out of his line of sight, Najid saw Saadri staring into space. He wondered if the brief exchange between he, Veronique, and Mary even registered with her. Najid gathered her about the waist and looked around the crowd to see if he could spot Bashan or his parents.

The interment progressed as smoothly as could be expected. People offered condolences and Saadri politely tolerated them. Najid led her back to Bashan's car to settle in for the sixty-minute ride to Brownsville from the Farmingdale cemetery. Saadri closed her eyes and welcomed a bit of rest as she nestled into Najid's firm and comforting embrace. Najid asked Bashan to prolong their trip. He sensed they would need the solitude.

They walked into the apartment well over an hour after leaving Farmingdale to bustling activity. Najid was more than perturbed by the amount of people, "You have got to be kidding me."

Teran echoed, "This place is wall-to-wall."

The woman he'd argued with at the funeral, Mary Clark, stood in the middle of the dining area holding down the fort and issuing commands, as if she had stepped into Ellen's shoes. It was then Najid realized his and Saadri's next area of battle. Mary needed to be removed from her self-delegated perch as matriarch and he knew it would not be easy nor would it be pretty.

Nevertheless, Saadri was his wife and he was solely responsible for her well-being. He would do what he needed to do in order to safeguard their marriage and Mary Clark had no role in it, Najid would never allow her to, especially after the disrespect she'd shown him. Najid held his mien with the older woman for Ellen and Saadri's sake, to the point of questioning whether he'd done something to offend her. The last straw was the funeral confrontation and the fact of Veronique stepping in to put the woman in her place verified things had gone far enough. Najid looked at Saadri, "Are you up to all of this drama right now? If not, they'll all just have to go."

"It's a repast baby; people are trying to pay their respects." Saadri touched Najid's arm and weakly nodded her head.

Bashan announced, "Fambily coming drough!" He took the rear as Najid escorted the small group to the back of apartment.

Damas stood in the doorway of his bedroom and watched their approach. "I hope no one calls the fire department. Good of you all to get here. Dri, vini Pe'r piti." Saadri walked into her father's arms and held him with strength quickly waning.

Najid unlocked he and Saadri's bedroom door and announced to the trio behind him, "Candy can come in here and lay down." He walked into the room, removed his suit jacket and hung it on the back of the door; Bashan and the ladies filed in after him. Teran reached for Bashan's jacket and hung it with Najid's as Bashan settled in a beige rocking chair and Veronique kicked off her shoes and reclined on an antique mahogany and beige brocade settee. Teran removed her shoes and nestled into Bashan's lap. The couple kissed one another as Veronique volleyed a quip, which they ignored. Najid shook his head at the scene and stepped in the hall where Damas and Saadri remained in their embrace. He watched them and felt his throat constrict, the two had gone through an awful experience helplessly watching Ellen die. He wanted to console his wife yet he knew father and daughter needed this time.

Saadri opened her eyes as Najid stood in the entrance of their bedroom. Concern was etched all over his face. She felt bad for having to be the one to place the lines of worry on his wrinkled brows but she was thankful he was there for her. She left her father's warmth and went to him, they looked into one another's eyes. Najid had been there for her throughout the entire ordeal of her mother's final days. She loved him more than she could express at that point. Saadri was about to share her feelings when Mary's voice broke the intimacy of their moment.

Mary grabbed Saadri's arm firmly, breaking the contact she had with Najid. "Go on in that room girl and rest your tired body. Don't think I didn't see how exhausted you were today. I'm going to make sure you eat something."

Najid made ready to lace into Mary when he felt a firm hand on his shoulder. He turned to face Damas' perceptive grin, "Our talk seems imminent. What about it?" Damas looked into the bedroom and saw Teran on Bashan's lap, "Come up for some air boy, it's time for the men to talk. Let's go. Get your last smooch and get your butt in here!" Najid laughed as Damas steered him into the adjacent bedroom. Bashan was on their heels and closed the door behind them.

Damas laid across his bed while the younger men sat in chairs placed in two corners of the room. When the door opened, Najid prayed to God for the strength not to strangle Mary. Both men turned and Saadri stood watching them. Najid sucked in a bit of air. Saadri seemed about to pass out, the stress had so taken its toll on her. "Baby, you should be laying down." He moved to her immediately. "Let us talk Candy and then I'm all yours, okay?" When she nodded Najid went to the door. "Terry, Nique! Come here!"

The sisters appeared at the door. Veronique questioned Najid as Teran sat beside Saadri. "Is there a reason you're yelling as if we are part of your stable Pimp Daddy?"

Damas shot her a look and she lowered her eyes. Najid spoke softly, "I need you both to look after my Candy while I talk with Pe'r. She doesn't need to be alone and she doesn't need Bloody Mary in her face either." Damas then shot a warning look at Najid who held his hands up in surrender.

Teran sprang into action, "Vini Saadri, let's lay on your bed together, okay?" She stood with Saadri to exit but moved after Veronique walked over and stood on the opposite side.

Over her shoulder Veronique commented, "Don't worry about Attila the Hun, I got something for her."

Damas commanded, "You most certainly do not."

Veronique shrank back, "Pe'r I am going to tell Mon mon Nadine, that's what I meant."

Najid looked at Damas and Bashan, the men burst into a snicker. They nodded as Damas spoke, "Oh this will be good and I should feel badly about wanting to see those sparks fly."

Najid finished his thought, "But you don't. Besides, you don't need to worry about that. Family has your back."

Damas nodded, "You're right. Are you fellas hungry? Terry, get Godzilla to make everyone a plate, for you and your sisters too. I want Saadri to eat something."

Veronique stated, "You know she is usually asleep before her head hits the pillow and she is dead on her feet now."

Damas shook his head, "She hasn't eaten in two days, make her eat then she can sleep. Dri, eat for your daddy baby, you hear me?" Saadri nodded as the ladies led her into the other bedroom.

Najid stepped into the doorway of the room, "You two take care of my baby for me. Close the door and lock it." He reiterated Damas' words, "Candy you should be hungry by now. I think you should eat." He looked back at Veronique since Saadri had not responded. "Get the witch to make you all plates, and when you have them, lock the door again."

"Aye aye Captain!" Veronique saluted and laughed when Najid shot a look at her. "You order me around and I get the look? Geesh!" She went into his bedroom.

Najid bellowed, "That's because you're a trip! I feel sorry for the man who marries you!" He stepped back into Damas' room and heard banging on the wall, he burst into laughter.

Bashan stood with both arms raised to the ceiling, "Dat gyal nuh easy!"

Damas shouted, "Arété sèk Veronique! Mo pa konné kòfè to kompotté kom ça!" The banging stopped and the fellas snickered. Damas continued, "I don't know why she acts like that, she's such a spitfire." You would think she is Nadine's daughter because she actually acts more like her than Teran. Teran acts more like Marceline, they say whatever they want and act as if no one should be upset with them or that they should suffer any consequences."

Bashan nodded as he listened. "Dat ah Teran. Suh much wi quarrel wen wi dated cah shi didn't tink bout wah shi sey. Mi dought ih was sum fantasy world but now mi kno ih dis type of entitlement or sup'm."

Damas nodded, "You got that right, it's an entitlement but we just didn't get the memo."

Najid laughed, "I guess not, huh? Well, I know you guys have some questions that only I can answer and I am sorry to say, you may not like what you hear…" He looked at the men with open palms and resolve.

Damas sat up and uttered, "Mondjé (my God) boy what have you done?"

Chapter 23

Najid began, "Pe'r I know I would not have been your choice for your daughter but-"

"That is not true, I have not gotten nor taken a chance to really know you to make a judgment one way or another; that applies to both of you. I do see that you are like a surrogate father for Saadri. It magnifies how I have messed things up for my girls. They sought and found in the two of you strength and devotion they did not receive from me. I have to live with that reality so I am in no position to say whether either of you is unsuitable, heck, I was unsuitable to be their father yet I had three baby girls looking at me for examples of manhood. Bare bones fellas, that's how I am." He rolled the sleeves of his shirt up and leaned forward in his seat. "My stuff is out there for you to see. Now let's talk."

Najid opened his palms, "You came and reestablished yourself quickly with your wife and daughters and I know that took a lot of energy, we were lower on the list of things to do."

"Inna time aal tings wuk demself out. Mi neva fret bout wi relationship. Wid men tings tek longa fi develop." Bashan rubbed his hands together as he spoke.

"I'm glad you both understand. So now here we are and I need to get to know my sons better; never had sons but glad to have them now. What I want is honesty between us and for us to be a support for one another. I know that will take time and testing but nothing like right now to get it started. What do you think?" Damas looked from Bashan to Najid and waited for their responses.

Bashan led by first disclosing his background "Mi am de babi fram an affair an neva kno ih til mi fada cum an met mi lass year. Mi mudda gi mi bodderation aal de while mi grow up. Nutten eva gud aalways Shani yuh nuh duh dis, Shani yuh nuh duh dat."

He then connected his past with he and Teran's relationship. "Wen mi saw Teran mi kno shi was de one ooman Jah mek fah mi own. Aal mi duh ah fah Teran an wi future fambily. Yet mi learn fi be a mon fram Crandall mi stepfada but mi fada mi ongle kno til lass year. Yuh mek tree fadas mi ave an dat aright wid mi cah mi know mi cud learn fram yuh as well." Bashan sat back in his chair and awaited a response.

"I'll be glad to know you too Bashan. Give you some tips on handling Teran because she is me and Nadine and I know she can be a handful." Damas clapped him on the knee and the two shared a laugh.

Najid grinned, "You have concerns about me Mr. Damas, I know."

"What happened to Pe'r? I do have concerns but like I said we have to start the trust somewhere."

Najid looked from Damas' encouraging smile, a smile he'd seen on his wife's face often, to Bashan's knowing smirk. He laughed, "Oh man, you two are a trip. You have talked before haven't you?"

Damas answered, "We have had the chance to touch base a few times, yes. Come on man, what's going on and how can we help? Saadri is sad a lot and worried over you. I see you come and be gone for days. That's no way to maintain your marriage, but I know you are already aware of that."

Bashan added, "Shim cum fi Baldwin an cry har yeye out ova yuh an wah shim tink yuh duh. Mi tole har not fi cum fi any conclusion shim nuh able fi prove bout wah yuh duh. Mi promise fi taak wid yuh but neva gat de time yuh gwon suh. Weh yuh guh an wah gwan mon? Mi help yuh eff mi cya."

Najid put his head in his hand, "I know you both are there for me so I won't beat around the bush. This thing is heavy and bigger than all of us so I have to go through this thing solo. I don't want to involve anyone else."

Damas focused on Najid's words, "You mean you are protecting us." Najid looked at him a moment before he nodded. "Good Lord boy, what have you gotten yourself into?" No one expected an answer.

Bashan sighed, "Wah bout Saadri? Wa'ppun wid har eff...? Wah yuh wan duh bout har?"

His answer came quickly, "I have money put away for her and I want her to go on with her life. When I first met Saadri she was maybe thirteen or fourteen, she was my brother's friend. I immediately asked him if she was his girl and when he said they were only friends I knew she had to be mine. She was the cutest, smartest, classiest little lady out here in these projects. She was here but not from here, you know what I mean?"

Bashan laughed, "Mi cyan seh dat fah Teran. Shi was here an fram here. Mi had fi wuk haad fi get dat way of tinking out of har. Still dere ah times shi cya guh bak fi dat way but mi affi remind har shi nuh dere no mo."

Damas laughed, "You know you're wife boy. I give you that. Sounds like you needed those tips sooner."

"But mi still welcome dem Pe'r. De wuk wid Teran nuh done, wi quarrel bout har temper just de oda night."

"B, I can't believe you haven't been able to tame her. You the man I thought." Najid clapped his hands.

Bashan snorted, "Dere's a process bredda an mi guh trough ih wid har. Consistence is de ansa."

They all laughed and Damas replied, "Yes, because they will consistently test your patience. All my girls' mothers are consistent in their way and they passed it down to their daughters. Teran goes at things like a raging bull so you have to play matador with her and tire her out before you can reason with her. Saadri sweetly and wisely wears you down until you give up but then you don't mind since she's so doggone gracious. Then there is Veronique who pushes you to the point of wanting to choke the daylights out of her then she flips it and acts like the martyr, the misunderstood martyr. God bless the man who marries her because I won't tolerate him hitting her so he'd better be able to handle that girl." More laughter ensued before the men settled down to hear Najid out.

"Oh man you too funny Pe'r but you have those girls of yours dead to rights. Look, I won't go through a long story here. I love Saadri and have loved that girl for the past five years. That's why she is my wife today. I did not come after her before she was ready to come out of high school. Before that time I did my thing and now some of what I was into has been harder than I thought to extricate myself from. Truthfully, I don't know how this might shake out but I am seeing it through. If things don't work out for me then I lived, loved the woman I wanted, got a chance to make my peace with God and can't be upset about how things turned out. What I want is for Candy to be taken care of so I have money set aside for her and an insurance policy. All I need is to know that you have my back in this and we are good. I have not put her in any danger, she is fine."

"Yuh ave mi wud Saadri ave a big bredda inna mi. Yuh know mi wife ah har twin and will mek sure Saadri is tek care of. Shim ah gud wid wi."

Damas rubbed a hand over his face. "This is heavier than I thought but know that we will take care of Saadri. You know I will do anything for my babies."

Nadine closed the bedroom door, livid. She walked into the living room and cleared her throat. "Good afternoon everyone. On behalf of my family I would like to thank you for your support today. We said goodbye to our mother, best friend, wife, and all the things Ellie was to so many people. At this time, we would like to have some privacy and reflect on our loved one as a family unit. We thank you again for your support and for now respecting our request for private time. We would also like to thank Zion Temple and Pastor Kent Sailor for all of their service to our family on this difficult day." As Nadine finished she looked around the room to ensure she had the attention of everyone. She moved toward the door and Butch, Bashan, Najid, and Damas followed. People filed pass them offering parting condolences as they smiled and gave thanks.

When the apartment cleared, Nadine prepared for the next round. Mary covered dishes on the table and spoke to the two other women with her. Nadine turned toward her, "Ladies, thank you for your assistance. We will finish this up and bring empty and cleaned dishes to the church by the Wednesday night service." All of them stopped and looked at Nadine.

Mary spoke, "We knew you all had a lot to deal with so we were trying to straighten up for you. Now since you are putting everyone out we'll take our leave."

Nadine walked over to the older, outspoken woman, "Miss Mary we thank you for your kindness to our family, for taking care of Ellie, and for organizing the repast. We will be able to manage from here and thank you for the house keys at this time."

Mary blustered as she removed the keys from her pocket, "Rest assured I did not take one thing from this house."

Nadine responded, "I never accused you of anything. We require the keys now because this next leg of the journey is ours to make. What I will say though is that we have not appreciated your treatment of our son Najid. If he in any way offended you then you should have said something to us and we would have straightened things out but to disrespect him, start an argument with him on the day he was burying his mother-in-law, and to get in the middle of he and his wife was not the right thing to do."

Before Mary could reply Damas stepped up and handed her an envelope, "We would like to thank you again for your services. You made Ellie's last days comfortable."

"I don't want your money! I didn't do anything for money." Mary recoiled.

Damas smiled, "Our gift to you is not meant to imply you did anything for money but to recognize your unselfish devotion to our loved one. Please take this as a token of our appreciation and use it however you deem fit. Ellie would have wanted you to have this."

At the mention of Ellie's name Mary softened and asked, "May I see Saadri before I go?"

Najid answered, "Saadri has really not been doing well through this. We have her in the room with her sisters resting for the first time in weeks. I will personally make sure she contacts you when she is feeling better."

Mary nodded, "Thank you, I would appreciate that and thank you for the gift." She held up the envelope, "I really wasn't expecting this." She and the ladies left the house and Damas gave Nadine a hug that lifted her petite frame off the ground.

Chapter 24

Late Summer 1985

Saadri sat at the kitchen table looking through brochures for local area colleges when the insistent knock drew her attention. She was surprised to see Margari Raenier waiting on the other side. "Mama Margi, come on in. I am surprised to see you. Have a seat. May I get you something to drink? I have a quarter strawberry and pineapple filled sheet cake I picked up from Mrs. Maxwell's Bakery the other day. Would you like a piece?"

Margi settled herself on the couch and Saadri could tell she was upset. She braced herself for more shocking news. "No baby, I don't want anything. I came to talk to you."

"Okay." Saadri sat beside Margi and waited for her to begin.

"I know you see the change in Najid. This time I think it's really bad. He's tried to move back in and had a fight with Jack and-"

Saadri started, "Move back in and a fight with Papa Jack?! When?! I don't believe this!"

Tears appeared in Margi's eyes as she spoke, "He and Jack had a bad argument about what he's out there doing. We found out he is not on Wall Street anymore. Jack confronted him about it and not being much of a husband to you. Najid told Jack he was grown and didn't have to explain his business. What did he say that to Jack for? Jack knocked him down and Najid flared up to the point where I got nervous. Jack put him out and there was nothing I could do about it. I was hoping he ended up back here even though I figured things weren't going well for you two either. I haven't heard from or seen him since that night and it's been over two weeks."

Saadri was stunned, "Mama Margi, he's not here. In fact, I rarely see him for us to live in the same apartment. This has been going on a few months now. There are days when I don't see him at all. I assumed he was upstairs with you but now that you're saying he's not, I don't know what to think."

Margi sniffled, "He has changed so much, and I don't recognize my own child anymore. We have always been so close. You came along and I saw a young man I could be proud of. Now those streets have claimed him again. I don't want to end up at my son's funeral or see him in jail the way they sentence these black boys."

Saadri felt her stomach lurch, "I tried to talk to him a few weeks ago and the truth is-"

Margi watched Saadri carefully, "What is it baby?"

"I had the strangest feeling that he was saying goodbye to me. We got into a huge fight when I confronted him about what he was doing."

Margi lowered her head. "Why would he be upset, you're his wife?"

Saadri shook her head, "That morning was the last time Najid attempted to be in the house with me. I hoped that if I backed off, he would get it together and come back to his senses. That's obviously not going to happen from what you've just told me."

Margi desperately grabbed Saadri's hand, "Baby, just pray for him, please. I know you pray so please keep him in your prayers. Jack has had it. He said Najid is a grown man and has to make as well as live by his choices. Jack plans to retire in the next three months and we are leaving New York for Texas. He gave Rasheen the opportunity to come with us and get into school or stay in New York and support himself."

"Wow! My father spoke to me about coming to live with him in Texas too. This must be a sign; I am seriously thinking about it, I need a break."

Margi smiled, "Saadri, a fresh start is just what you need. You don't owe Najid anything and I want the best for you because you are a good girl. You were always a cut above the rest of the kids around here. Sad to say, you are also a cut above my son. Move on with your life and be happy. Get out of here and don't look back."

Saadri cried, "I can get away for a while but how can I not look back? He's my husband. I took those vows seriously even if he didn't."

Margi hugged Saadri, "You're a fine woman Saadri. I am behind whatever decision you make and I want you to know the Raeniers are your family no matter what."

Long after Margi left, she pondered their conversation.

Two Weeks Later

Saadri sat immobilized as Jack Raenier maneuvered his car toward Brookdale Hospital. Margi called forty-five minutes earlier and told her Najid was shot in a narcotics bust and was in the hospital under police security. Two bullets were surgically removed from the left side of his mid-section. The family would be allowed to see him after he was moved into a room. Saadri dressed and stood outside the building well ahead of the Raeniers.

Rasheen held her hand protectively as they waited for their turns in the hall outside Najid's room. He spoke in soft, reassuring tones. "This has to turn out okay. Ace is smarter than this."

Saadri knew the words Rasheen spoke were more for him. "Rasheen, do you know what he's been doing over the past few months? Did you know when he left his job?"

Rasheen shook his head, "There is a lot I don't know about Ace, he does that on purpose. That's why I am saying things are not adding up. He's a lot smarter than this."

Saadri sighed, "Well Rah, things change and people change, you know?"

Rasheen was about to speak when his mother and father entered the hall. Jack spoke, "You can go on in there." Rasheen faltered from his father's stiff response. Things were really bad. He went inside.

Saadri waited fifteen minutes but it felt more like an hour. She didn't know what to say but she did know she had to see Najid. She stood, took a deep breath, and pushed the door open. Najid was hooked up to several monitors and a catheter ran along the bottom rail of his bed. Her breath caught, never had she seen the man she loved more vulnerable. She did love him and she missed him terribly. Her eyes teared but she quelled their flow. Her heart would have melted had she not looked into the displeasure evident on Najid's face. Who was the man reacting to her as if she were intruding? Saadri proceeded to sit in the chair next to his bed. Najid would not make eye contact.

Najid started as he watched Saadri enter the room. She was not supposed to see him like this. He watched her staring at him with question-filled eyes and it was almost hard for him to do what he knew had to be done. Najid focused above her head, at the top of the chair, everywhere else, and sighed, "So what am I supposed to do? Throw a parade because you decided to grace my hospital room with your presence?" The pain he saw when he looked in her face almost made his breath catch, he had to look away.

If Najid had slapped her face, it wouldn't have felt worse. Saadri lost all of the strength she mustered. His tone reduced her to a pleading she couldn't control. "Why are you doing this? What have I done to deserve this?"

Najid closed his eyes; he still had not faced her. Finally, he turned his attention toward Saadri. "What do you want me to say Saadri? It is what it is."

Saadri touched his arm, "But why Najid? You could get a lot of time for drug trafficking. What am I supposed to do without you around?" Saadri was scared, mostly of Najid's drastic demeanor.

Najid firmly removed her hand from his arm. "You go on with your life, that's what you do. Hook up with a good college boy and go on with your life."

Saadri was riled, "Just like that? After all we've been through, I'm supposed to go on just like that?" She snapped her fingers for emphasis.

Najid's eyes narrowed. "What else do you want me to say?! All of you know the deal; it's right here in your faces. There's nothing for me to explain. It is what it is."

Saadri knew she would get no further with Najid. The best thing was to show support. "Najid, what do you want me to do for you? Should I get money from the account and hire a lawyer? We can get through this baby, please don't fight me."

Najid spoke in the softest tone he used since her arrival, "I am not the man you need. It's time to find someone else Saadri."

Saadri implored, "Najid you are my husband. We are supposed to be together until we die- now how am I supposed to forget my vows and find someone else?"

Najid answered, "I'll give you a divorce."

Saadri cried, "Why Najid? I love you -"

He cut her off, "Love someone else Saadri." Najid gingerly turned his body away from Saadri and dropped off to sleep.

Saadri was near hysterics by the time she reached her apartment. Rasheen wanted to stay with her but she knew she wasn't able to deal with company. Thankfully, her father was in Texas, she needed the solitude to understand the way things unraveled.

November

Saadri sat in her living room stunned; Damas ranted in Creole. Spread before her on the coffee table was a picture of she and Najid taken by her mother and divorce papers sent to her from his lawyer. In the picture he held her protectively and the smile on her face said that she was happy. Her heart ached as she looked at Najid's slow smile and powerful presence. Things changed so abruptly. How could she go from the woman Najid loved to yesterday's news? "We leave for Texas in January, for good. You can no longer stay here; you don't need to be here anymore." Damas poured himself another drink, went into the bedroom and slammed the door. Saadri cried until her throat was raw and she could muster no more air with which to sob. She sat late into the night trying to make sense of the world that came crashing down around her.

Saadri lay in the upstairs bedroom of Teran and Bashan's Long Island home weeping on and off for the better part of four hours. The smell of food drove her from the room. When she entered the kitchen she caught Bashan telling Teran to be strong for her sake. "She doesn't have to be strong for me. I had a feeling for months something was going to happen. I prayed and cried and prayed some more for God not to take my husband and He honored that. Najid is still alive; going to jail probably saved his life." She walked over to the stove and looked at the lasagna. "Sè please tell me Nonk sent madlènn." (Sister please tell me Uncle sent andouille sausages)

Teran smiled, "Saadri Nonk sent madlènn."

Her eyes glistened, "And you put it in the lasagna?" Teran nodded. "Mèsi Sinyè!"

Teran got up to get Saadri something to drink while she slid into the vacated row, said grace, made the sign of the cross, and answered, "I could use a break from all of this mess. Maybe it's time for a more permanent change of scenery. There is nothing keeping me in Brownsville anymore. You know Pe'r has been transitioning back to Texas and after this mess with Najid, he told me he wanted to take me with him. I do know that when he leaves I am not staying in that apartment. He only stayed because of Mon mon being too sick to leave New York. Did you know Pe'r had a house in Texas? Anyway, I have decided to go and live with him."

Teran sat next to her and gave her a cup of juice. "I'd heard something about Texas but I didn't know he actually kept a house there. We all can visit but you can't leave me here by myself."

Saadri looked at her sister, "Says who? I have nothing holding me here anymore and you have your husband," Saadri pointed toward Bashan, "not to mention all of your family. I most certainly am leaving New York. Najid has made his stance clear."

Bashan sensed tension rising, "Wah mi wife meant fi seh is dat shi will miss yuh an mi will too. Yuh nuh affi rush off too fast yuh know? Wi ave nuff room here at de ouse fah yuh an wi wud luv fi ave yuh around fah a while." He winked at Teran.

Saadri looked between the grinning couple, "What aren't you telling me? Terry? Teeerrrryyyy?"

Teran sucked her teeth, "You always have to spoil everything! I'm pregnant."

"Yes! I knew it! Did you tell Nique yet?" Teran shook her head and Saadri clapped her hands. "Hah! I told Nique you two wouldn't last a year. I told her 'Teran will be knocked up before her first anniversary.' Scoot over girl so I can get to the phone! Haha!"

Teran stood and Saadri ran over to the phone mounted to the wall closet to the refrigerator. She called Veronique and announced Teran's pregnancy to which the oldest sister asked for Teran to get on the phone. She blasted the youngest for costing her fifty dollars before she congratulated the couple and promised to visit before Teran's due date.

Chapter 25

January 1986

Nadine made a beef stew, biscuits, and a scratch pound cake that everyone devoured before setting about the apartment packing for Damas' return to Texas. Saadri decided to stay with Teran and Bashan for a while.

Damas rubbed his stomach, "Butch I am glad you are back because Nay is so much nicer and domesticated now."

Nadine threw a cloth at him. "Just say thank you and shut up."

Butch laughed and shook his head. "I still don't know how you did it." He pointed to Teran.

Damas answered, "Teran looks like me so you know I took charge. First I had to get the chair and the whip." The room exploded with laughter but became hysterical when Nadine rolled her eyes and walked into the back of the house with Talib in tow.

Teran responded, "You know she is going to get you back, don't you?"

Damas rubbed his wet eyes, "I wouldn't have it any other way. That girl is fire and ice."

Ayana commented, "Pe'r, leave my mother alone. She cooked for you."

Damas grabbed Ayana and sat her on his lap, "Poupe' if I would have just said thank you, she would have said something smart. Now am I right?" Ayana and he started snickering. He pretended to spank her and said, "Go on and help your mon mon fiy." She jumped up and went to the back of the house laughing.

Butch stretched, "Okay let's get going before the –itis sets in. Then I won't do a thing." He put on the radio and turned to Damas, "Hey man where is your jazz? Did you pack it away yet?"

"No sir! Look in that crate to your left and load them up on the record player. These kids don't know good music." Damas stood and rolled up his sleeves so he too could begin work. Miles Davis filled the air and the men gave each other an "Outta sight!" and slapped five before working in their respective areas.

The Raeniers were scheduled to leave within a week of learning Najid accepted a plea bargain and would be in jail for four to six years. Rasheen sat in Saadri's sparse apartment shaking his head. "Your dad wasn't playing! You cleaned this place out!"

Saadri laughed, "It wasn't too hard once we decided upon what to sell or give away or store. I go to the rent office on Monday morning then I am out of here for good. You know, I don't even think I'll miss it Rah."

Rasheen sat pensively, "Are you talking about the place or the people?"

"Oh Rah." Saadri reached across the kitchen table, one of the few pieces of furniture left, and touched Rasheen's arm. "You know I'll miss you and the family…"

Hearing her voice trail off made Rasheen sorry he forced her admission. "I'm sorry Saadri. I know you still love him. How can I help you?"

Saadri shook her head, "Rah, I couldn't ask for a better brother. You have always been a friend…There's nothing for me to do except give Najid some space. His last words to me were to love someone else. I still can't believe he said that to me. To top that he had divorce papers sent to the house."

"You have to be lying to me! What? Saadri, I still don't think things add up. All of this is so unlike Ace; I have never known my brother not to think long and hard about something before he pursued it. He pushed everybody away from him. It's like he was trying to keep us from something."

"Rah, I have been thinking about that ever since we visited the hospital. When I was in the room, I could sense Najid's heart wasn't saying the same thing as his mouth. I could feel his torment when he looked at me with those steely eyes and told me to leave him alone. But what can I do about any of it now? He said what he wanted, quite clearly if I may add. I have no other choice but to leave him alone for a while. He doesn't want me around and it hurts like hell."

Rasheen sighed, "The two of you are supposed to be together. You were getting a house out on Long Island one minute, the next minute he was acting like he couldn't stand to be around you. Something was up. People just don't change that drastically. Something was definitely up. Plus, he won't accept mail and we had to go through major changes to even find out where he was. My father got a friend to do him a favor. Ace didn't even want us to know where he was."

Saadri agreed, "Rah, Najid was into something bigger than all of us and Pe'r thinks organized crime has to be at the root."

Rasheen looked Saadri in the eye. "My parents and I have gone over this too. Ace was into something heavy. We decided that if he went through all of this trouble to distance himself, he was trying to protect us. You have the right idea Dri, just leave it alone for now."

They sat in silence before Rasheen added, "Do you think you will be able to forgive him?"

Saadri sighed. "Rah, I can't sit here and say I am not hurt and even angry about what has happened. I was looking forward to spending my life with Najid and now I can't because of wrong choices he made. Do I hate him? No. Can I forgive him? Yes, because he's already paying, just like we are, for trying to be the tough guy. He is so intelligent, I wished he could have gotten his life together sooner, that's all."

Rasheen looked at Saadri in amazement, "How can you do that? You are always so strong. That's what made me respect you so much. I know that is one of the reasons why my brother fell in love with you." Saadri watched Rasheen carefully. "Rah, I can do that because of Christ's love for me. God is a forgiving God. He forgives us of our shortcomings."

Rasheen spoke, "You really live like that. I haven't seen too many people who say they love God really live like that. Is it hard for you?"

Saadri smiled, "No. I take it one day at a time. God has a purpose for us and when we get to know Him, He reveals that purpose, guides us, and keeps us from a lot of craziness when we stay in relationship with Him."

"How do you do that? You make it sound like going out with God or something."

Saadri nodded, "Exactly, God should be most important in your life. He'll give you a mate and take care of all your needs but you have to serve Him first."

"Yeah, but you have to have your stuff together to do all of that." Rasheen shook his head negatively.

"No Rah, it's not about having your stuff together because if you could get it together by yourself then you wouldn't need God. God wants you to come to Him when you realize you are messed up. Then He takes you and straightens you out. He changes you in His time and He will take care of you and teach you and most of all, use you to help others."

Rasheen was pensive. "Do you think He would accept me like this? I mean, I haven't been a thug or anything but I haven't paid God much attention either. And my brother, do you think after what he has been involved in, God would accept him too?"

Saadri smiled, "The answers to both of those questions are 'Yes.' God will accept you because you ask Him to, just like He accepted your brother when he asked Him to. Would you like to ask God to accept you?"

Rasheen nodded. "Yeah; I think I am ready to do that."

Saadri led him in the Prayer of Salvation, said a prayer of intercession over him and promised to escort him to a store where he could get some materials to begin his studies.

Later in the evening, they went up to the Raenier apartment for Saadri to get the new address. When they walked in the door Margi Raenier quickly wiped her face. Jack Raenier was in the kitchen wearing a disgusted expression.

Rasheen expressed his concern, "What's the matter mommy? Why are you crying?"

Margi stood from one of three chairs arranged in the dining area, "Hey Saadri baby, how are you?" Rasheen was about to reiterate when Margi answered, "I heard you boy. I was thinking about your brother. We're going all the way to Texas and he's up here. It's hard to leave him like this."

Saadri was about to speak when Jack erupted, "Yeah and I told her to stop worrying about him because he's not worried about us. He will find his way. Najid always did just what he wanted to do. I'm going to Texas with a clear conscience."

Saadri had to say something to discharge the air. "I am praying that everything will turn out okay in the end. It's so funny that we're all going to Texas."

Jack spoke, "That is something else isn't it? This big old world is small after all. It will be good to get to know Damas better. What part will you be in?"

"I will be living in Mesquite, at least for another six months. My father wants me to go to college and live on campus."
Jack shook his head, "He's right. You need to have time to be young. You had a lot on your plate. I'm sorry my son added to your grief. Believe me, he wasn't raised like that."

"I know Papa Jack. Najid made his bed hard and he is sleeping in it right now. I really believe that he'll come around sooner or later."

Her statement made everyone in the room pensive. Rasheen broke the silence, "Dad, how far is Mesquite from San Antonio?"

Jack looked upward before responding. "Saadri you will be about four hours away from us. Don't forget us now. You come and visit, okay? We are still your family."

Rasheen added, "Yes, even though Najid is acting like a lunatic right now? Did you know he served her with divorce papers?"

Jack and Margi voiced their disbelief before Jack added, "No matter what Saadri, we are your family. Don't be estranged from us. We love you like our own because you are. Najid has lost his mind."

Margi added, "You are our daughter Saadri. We've gone through so much craziness together: Najid's bad decisions; the false alarm with Aida and her baby; your mother's illness and death; and now this. I don't want to lose contact with you, it would be too much. Once you get yourself settled with Damas, I want you to promise that you will come and spend some time with us."

Her heart went out to Margi; she understood it was harder for her to deal with because Najid was closer to his mother. "Mama Margi, I would love to come and visit all of you in San Antonio. I'm sure my dad will be more than happy to come and visit you too." Saadri didn't stay long, they exchanged addresses, hugs and kisses and then she left to pursue the next stage of her life.

Epilogue

Six months later.

Saadri relaxed in the larger of two living areas in the gorgeous, immaculate, upscale, Mesquite home. Damas hired a custom decorator who created a tropical theme in the room that backed up to a greenbelt and creek for privacy. The room was her favorite; Damas often came home to find her lounging in a chaise peering out of the bow window. She enjoyed the view and celebrated her acceptance into Agricultural and Mechanical University. In the fall, she would be off to College Station and staying on campus. The rays streaming into the area warmed her skin as she closed her eyes. Her mind wandered to Najid.

Saadri thought of him constantly during her six-month hiatus. Damas was correct; she needed time to sort through her thoughts, mourn and process the events that transpired prior to her relocation. With her eyes shut, Saadri could feel Najid's presence. Her mind's eye flashed varied scenes of their too short time together. His lips crushing hers, his penetrating eyes, their last night together… When Saadri opened her eyes they were cloudy with her tears. She wondered how he was doing and why she wasn't permitted to contact him. Saadri also wondered why Najid went to jail; what caused the drastic change in his behavior? Again, Rasheen's suspicions surfaced. What was he hiding?

The phone rang and Saadri was grateful for the distraction. Rasheen announced his matriculation into San Antonio University. He invited her and Damas down to the family home for a celebratory barbecue.

"We'll see you this weekend." Saadri disconnected and smiled to herself. Rasheen was adjusted and ready to move on. The Raeniers were settled in San Antonio and she was living with her father and on her way to college. Mr. Raenier had been correct; Najid had to live with his decisions.

Never, since the sweeping changes she endured, had Saadri felt the resolve she felt in her favorite room. She stood and walked into the kitchen. It was a cook's dream with an island, breakfast bar, cook top, wall ovens, and separate eating area. Saadri opened the refrigerator and retrieved the ingredients for the night's dinner. As she began to prepare the meal, she thought about her father's home. Her father achieved things beyond the realities of life in East New York and Saadri knew she wanted to achieve that reality as well. She hummed a tune very popular at Zion Temple. Tears of joy spilled from her eyes as she sliced zucchini and squash for stewing. Saadri was never much of a singer but she opened her mouth, "I just want to thank you Lord!" Indeed, she had much to be thankful for. Her life may have had some turbulence but she was sure better days were ahead.

Saturday morning, Damas made quick work of Highway 35 E and had them in San Antonio by noon. Saadri was excited; she'd not seen the Raeniers in at least six months. They turned onto 8th Street, entered the Royal Oaks subdivision and had no problem finding number 403 on the right.

Margi Raenier opened her front door as soon as they turned into the driveway. Saadri jumped out before Damas cut the engine. Margi stepped out into the Texas sun and Saadri was taken with how young and vibrant she looked. The ladies bounded toward one another and hugged tearfully; Damas walked up behind them with a smile on his face.

Margi relinquished Saadri and hugged him, "I know this must look like a soap opera to you Damas. You two come on in. Saadri, I missed you so much. You have to visit more often. I was used to the talks we had back in New York."

Saadri concurred, "I know. I never knew how much I missed seeing you until I saw you. Where's Rah Rah?"

Margi laughed, "He can't wait to see you either. I had to send him to pick up some things for me at the market, we had people coming and everything needed to be straight. Believe me; he will be upset about missing your arrival. That boy would probably have been standing in this driveway." The women laughed as Margi led the way into the house.

Jack called out from the back of the house. "That you boy? I need my sauce. Those ribs are looking good and ready to be glazed!"

Margi responded, "Jack! Saadri and Damas are here!"

Jack walked into the entry area. "Hey girl, come here!" Saadri walked quickly into his outstretched arms and was not disappointed by the hug she received. Jack held her at arms- length. "Looks like Texas agrees with you girl. You look like you are finally getting some meat on those bones. That's good; in New York you were a little toothpick. I like this new you."

Damas reached over and gave the customary handclasp to Jack. "I told her moving here would be the best thing for her. You know I couldn't leave my baby alone in New York. I would have worried myself sick."

Jack nodded, "Thank God she listened. I wouldn't have wanted her to stay either. Look man; come on out back with me. I got those ribs on and if Rasheen doesn't get back here with my sauce we're going to have some fireworks. We have some more family coming through here and they will be looking for my ribs. That boy was always too slow for my liking." The men laughed as they headed for the back yard.

Saadri looked at Margi who was grinning, "Girl, I am so glad you're here. Let me show you the house."

The two-story house had four bedrooms with walk-in closets in addition to two and one half baths. There was also a living room, separate dining room, loft, family room, and game room. The master bedroom was huge and boasted a sunken tub and separate shower. The Raenier home also had two-zone central air conditioning, ceiling fans, two-zone central heat, a water softener, and a central vacuum system.

Margi led Saadri, after the grand tour inside, to the back yard. Saadri could not contain her shock over the size. Jack looked up at her and smiled, "This is Texas baby-girl! Everything is big in Texas! We have four acres, a long way from Brownsville, isn't it?"

Saadri was about to answer when she heard, "Saadri! Dri! You here girl?! You better come give me some love girl!"

Saadri's head darted in the direction of the voice as Rasheen appeared in the kitchen doorway. "Rah Rah!" She ran to meet him and he caught her mid air, kissing and hugging her.

"Girl, it's so good to see you! Look at you; you look like Texas is treating you right." Rasheen held Saadri for close inspection.

Saadri laughed, "Well Texas has been good to you too pardner!" She stroked his newly grown goatee. Rasheen stroked it and posed. They laughed together and headed toward the house.

Jack called, "Wait before you two disappear. Saadri's daddy is here and you haven't even said 'boo' to the man and you are running off with his daughter. And where's my sauce! I'm over here trying to make my ribs and you are out running all over town." Rasheen laughed as he walked toward his father, handed him the sauce, and greeted Damas who watched with an amused expression. Rasheen then turned and grabbed Saadri by the hand.

"Let's get out of here before they want something else." Rasheen whispered conspiratorially and led them around the side of the house to his car. A blue and gray Camaro greeted them. He smiled at Saadri, "See my baby? She's pretty, aint she?"

Saadri answered, "Yes she is and I bet all the ladies want a ride." Rasheen raised his hands in a gesture of surrender, "What can I say? I am not in the business of disappointing the ladies." Saadri swatted his arm. He chuckled good-naturedly, "Hey-hey, don't damage the merchandise girl. I am a hot commodity here in Atascosa County." They laughed before Rasheen continued, "Do you want to take a drive or hang out around here?"

Saadri spoke, "I just got off the road. I would rather just hang out around here for a while and enjoy your company."

Rasheen answered, "Okay, follow me." They went toward the backyard and passed the adults who sat listening to sixties favorites and laughing. Rasheen led them to a gazebo surrounded by a crop of trees. Inside the décor was festive. Rasheen switched on the ceiling fan. "Dad always wanted a place just like this and he got it. It makes you think dreams can come true doesn't it?"

Saadri sat on a floral rattan sofa and enjoyed the breeze created by the ceiling fan. "Yes, I am glad too. It gives us something to strive for."

Rasheen walked behind a custom circular bar and poured Saadri and himself a beverage from a pitcher of pink lemonade chilling in the refrigerator before sitting on the rattan sofa. "So, Miss Saadri, what should we be striving for?"

Saadri turned toward Rasheen, "We should strive to finish college in three years."

Rasheen thought about it as he walked over with the drinks. He sat down before taking Saadri's hand, "It's a deal, we do it in three… or at least we try."

The two burst into laughter.

Series Description

Damas Buard, the progenitor, leaves Natchitoches Parish and the Cane River to attend New Orleans' Xavier University as a business major. He acquiesces to family plans - Marceline St. Amants, his intended fiancé, will matriculate with him. Not even the Buards or St. Amants could imagine the impact demure, petite Ellen Weston has on Damas. Nor could they imagine the attraction between him and the brash musician Nadine Scott. Far more unimaginable is the lengths their pampered Marceline (Merci) goes to keep her man. However, storms can produce beauty, as they all find out.

Meet the Buard sisters and the men who love them. Veronique, a green-eyed, golden-haired bombshell is the oldest. She is the daughter born to prim socialite Marceline St. Amant. She is a spitfire who is brash, unafraid, and unapologetic, except in matters of the heart. When she falls in love with Tavis Cordery fire meets earth and the burn is palpable.

Saadri, caramel complexioned with green and hazel eyes, is the level-headed middle daughter. Born to devout Ellen Weston, she lives by her faith and navigates her blended family well. She usually sets the proper example and does the right thing. When she falls in love with the neighborhood bad boy (Najid Raenier) the family and Saadri are never the same.

Teran is Saadri's *twin*; it's hard to believe they don't share the same mother. (Although, their mothers were best friends.) The youngest daughter is as spoiled, selfish, and impulsive as she is beautiful. She is a product of the combustible pairing of Nadine Scott and Damas. Bashan Watts is a self-assured, possessive, and demanding young man who is not put off by Teran's demeanor. As their relationship progresses Teran blossoms into a mature young woman.

The Buard family will make you cackle, cry, and commiserate. They all have a story – shared and individual.

Series Titles

Decisions (Saadri)	Book One	Summer 2017
Destinies (Teran)	Book Two	TBA
Determinations (Saadri)	Book Three	TBA
Definitions (Veronique)	Book Four	TBA
Detours (Veronique)	Book Six	TBA
Dalliances (Damas)	Book Five	TBA

About the Author

Stephanie Dunlap-Holloman is a native New Yorker and was educated in the gifted programs of NYC Board of Education. There she discovered her love of writing and received numerous writing awards. On the post-secondary level Stephanie had two poems published in her college's magazine. Along with writing, Stephanie has a love of learning. She holds a bachelor's degree from Hunter College, a master's degree from Adelphi University and completed doctoral work at Walden University (ABD.) She recently began a Master's of Fine Arts Writing program at Lindenwood University. As a twenty-seven year veteran educator, Stephanie currently teaches high school English but has been a school administrator, program director/coordinator, department chair, college instructor, and has taught on the preschool, elementary, and middle school levels.

Stephanie decribes herself an educator by vocation and calling. She is also a licensed and ordained minister who pastors a church – Kingdom Celebration Center-Hampton Roads in Hampton, Virginia with her husband Frank. Stephanie holds a certificate in Professional Life Coaching from Light University and is a former member of the American Association of Christian Counselors. Stephanie hails from a long line of pastors/ministers and educators. She is dedicated to helping others become better than they thought they could become and has been active in ministry for the past twenty years. She is the proprietor of MyVoice LLC – a company dedicated to helping others recognize, reach, and bring to fruition their potential. She and her husband have three children and two granddaughters and one grandchild expected in January 2018.